A Prayer for the Dying

A Prayer for the Dying

A NOVEL

Stewart O'Nan

HENRY HOLT AND COMPANY

NEW YORK

Henry Holt and Company, Inc.
Publishers since 1866
115 West 18th Street
New York, New York 10011

Henry Holt® is a registered trademark
of Henry Holt and Company, Inc.

Published in Canada by Fitzhenry & Whiteside Ltd.,
195 Allstate Parkway, Markham, Ontario L3R 4T8.

Library of Congress Cataloging-in-Publication Data
O'Nan, Stewart, 1961–
A prayer for the dying: a novel / Stewart O'Nan.—1st ed.
p.   cm.
ISBN 0-8050-6147-9 (HB: alk. paper)
I. Title
PS3565.N316P73   1999   98-39613
813'.54—dc21

Henry Holt books are available for special promotions and
premiums. For details contact: Director, Special Markets.

First Edition 1999

DESIGNED BY MICHELLE MCMILLIAN

Printed in the United States of America
All first editions are printed on acid-free paper.∞

1   3   5   7   9   10   8   6   4   2

The author would like to acknowledge his great debt to Michael Lesy,
whose *Wisconsin Death Trip* inspired this book.

*It shall never be said that my sorrow
has hardened me toward others.*

Glenway Wescott

⁓

*There is no escape in a time of plague.
We must choose to either love or to hate God.*

Albert Camus

A Prayer for the Dying

1

High summer and Friendship's quiet. The men tend the shimmering fields. Children tramp the woods, wade the creeks, sound the cool ponds. In town, women pause in the heavy air of the millinery, linger over bolts of yard goods, barrels of clumped flour. The only sound's the freight drumming through to the south, tossing its plume of cinders above the treetops, the trucks clicking a mile off. Then quiet, the buzz of insects, the breathless afternoon. Cows twitch and flick.

You like it like this, the bright, languid days. It could stand to rain, everyone says, the sawdust piles at the mill dry as powder, the great heaps of slash in the woods dangerous, baked to tinder, but there's something to the heat, the way it draws waves from tarpaper, stifles sound, closes town in. Winter was full of chimney fires and horses frozen on the plank road, and spring was hard, with the baby, but Marta's almost back to herself now, her garden thick, tomatoes fist-sized. Except Millie and Elsa Sullivan going at it with their flatware, and Mrs. Goetz passing in church, you haven't had much business of late, which is fine with you.

Not that you mind earning your money, but when folks have need of you it's someone's misfortune one way or the other. The undertaking's easy; being a constable is hard. When you put them together it can be too much, though that's only happened once since you've been back. And you got through that fine, did the Soderholms proud. With his head cocked on the pillow and his hair combed just so, you couldn't see where his brother conked him, and Eric, for his part, went easy, even came to the funeral in irons and his Sunday suit. You led him up to the casket for his last respects.

"I didn't mean it so hard," he said, not really sorry, still mad at him.

It was about a dog. Arnie threw it in the river above the mill dam to see if it would drown. It didn't, but by then it was too late to save either of the Soderholm brothers. It was just a plain rock, you picked it up in one hand, weighed it like an egg. Cain and Abel, you thought—your mother's love of Bible stories bubbling up—then thought it didn't fit. It was an accident, two good boys like that. When you told Marta, she cried.

The marshal who rode the mail stage up from Madison shook his head like it figured, a dying old lead town like Friendship. He squinted at the empty storefronts in judgment—*The Marquette County Record,* the First Bank of Wisconsin. You had the one brother in the cell and the other on a block in the icehouse, sawdust stuck to his jaw. You had the rock in a cheese box and the boy's confession ready for the marshal to take back to the capital. He was surprised you'd made such a nice job of Arnie's skull.

"You do anything else?" he asked.

"Preach a little," you said, trying not to sound proud. He wasn't really interested, only joking, so you didn't go into how you see all three as related, ways to give praise and thanks for this paradise. He wasn't that kind of man—he would have laughed at you. Others around town do, some kiddingly. It's all right. They'll all come to you someday, and they know you'll do right by them. It's a contract, an honor, you tell them. Friendship's my town, you say, and they think you're too serious, too sentimental, a fool. They think the war did something to you. Maybe so, but for the good, you think. That kind of talk doesn't temper your fondness for them. It's not just the job that makes you responsible. It *is* your town, they *are* your people, even the Hermit sitting in his dingy cave, his ducks setting up a racket if anyone comes near.

Today they send for you, or Old Man Meyer sends his littlest, Bitsi. She comes running, kicking up dust, getting her stockings dirty. "Sheriff Hansen! Sheriff Hansen!"

You're standing on the stairs outside, ignoring the big bay hitched outside of Fenton's dipping at the water trough. That's the one thing you'll admit is strange about you: you don't like to be around horses anymore. It's understandable, having had to eat them during the siege, to burrow into their warm, dead guts for cover, but you don't talk about that, or only to Marta, who'd never let it slip. It's come so no one asks why you ride the bicycle or pump the handcar along the rusty company spurs in the backwoods. The old hands must explain it to the newer immigrants—the Norwegians come to join family, the Poles who step off the stage looking stunned, the Cornish unaware there's nothing left to mine here.

Bitsi tackles your leg, hauls on your arm, too winded to get anything out. "Pa said come. Pa said come quick."

"Whoa, whoa," you say. It could be anything, nothing. Old Meyer's back pasture butts up against the Holy Light Colony, and the last few weeks he's had you out about people wandering through the woods at night with lit candles. It's a worry with everything so dry, but Meyer's real objection is with the Colony itself. It's new, mostly city folk, led by a man named Chase. The place runs back into the hills; Chase bought up the old Nokes claim—the mansion, the camp, everything. People say he preaches the Last Times. They say he leads services in the mines at night, that he shares his disciples' wives, that he eats nothing but unleavened bread, like some desert prophet, some wild-eyed stylite. You've met him once, and he seemed reserved, well-dressed, soft-spoken. You're unsure what you think of him, a fact you pride yourself on. It defines you, this willingness to hear all sides, love everyone. You've stopped believing in evil. Is that a sin? You know what your mother would say, but justice needs to be fair-handed, the dead deserve your compassion. It's your job to understand, to forgive, not simply your custom.

You kneel beside Bitsi so you're face to face. "Now slow down. What is it, honey?"

"Pa says there's a dead man."

"Someone from the Colony?"

"Pa found him back of the beehive. You gotta come."

You fit her on the handlebars and set off, wobbly, then straighten out. It's been so dry the roads are ground down flat, a treat after the frost heaves, the muds of April. Bitsi's never been on a bike before, and she's laughing, her fingers clenched white. You fly down halls of high, still barley. You cross the shadowy box of Ender's bridge, break into blinding sunlight. Behind you in town, steam boils up from the mill, sits thick as clotted cream in the bright sky. The church bell calls noon, the sound flat and weak in the heat. Not a swallow of air, just the shrill of hidden cicadas, grasshoppers popping up. A single cloud sails on the horizon, as if cut adrift.

The Meyer boys are in the garden, hoeing, twins in matching overalls. Marcus and Thaddeus. Twins. You're having a hard enough time with just Amelia, her all-night colic. Marta's tired all the time. Doc Guterson says it's normal, but that's no comfort. The Meyer boys stop and smile, polite. When they tip their straw hats, you can see where their tans stop, their foreheads bright as whitewash.

"Sheriff," they say. Your real title's constable, but only Marta ever calls you that, and only in bed.

"Boys."

"Pa's out back," one says, and you look to the other as if it's his turn. He grins blankly. You tip your hat, obliged, and Bitsi leads you past them.

Old Meyer's behind the house, scraping honeycomb into a bowl. His netting is thrown back, and a single bee sits on one cheek like a tear. He points the dripping knife at the treeline.

"Back there's a young fella dead, I don't know who."

"Tramp?" you guess, because it's been a hard year, a lot of men moving through, looking for work.

"Could be. Look like he's in the war by his get-up."

That's usually a clue; a lot of men never went home. Six years and they're still pitching and striking camp, marching at dawn.

"What do you think happened?" you ask.

"Couln't say. Din't look at him that hard, just saw he's dead, kinda green around the mouth."

"How far back's he in?"

"Just keep going straight," Old Meyer says, pointing the knife. "You'll find him."

Meyer's right. After a minute of picking through prickers, the heavy reek of rendered fat clamps around you like smoke. In a strange way, it's almost welcome; after the relief of the siege, your regiment had the job of searching for casualties, and this familiar smell in the middle of a Kentucky swamp meant some mother would get her son back.

This isn't so different. The man you come across is lying belly-down beside the smudge of a dead campfire. It's gone all night, the stones cracked and blackened. The cuffs of his private's blues are frayed white, the buttons missing. He's not green, more yellow, but definitely young—your age, no more than thirty, and beardless. You don't see any wounds. His face is so drawn, the eyes so deeply sunken, that for a moment you think of prisoners, starvation, yet that would take days. This looks quick, one minute sitting on the log, the next pitching over. Dropped from behind, coldcocked. You think of Eric Soderholm and his stone, the dog in the water. You wonder if it barked, if the boys could hear it over the falls.

Under a fern lies the same tin cup that rattled at your hip for three years. He's got the same jacket, the same belt, the same cap you came home in.

You squat and sniff the cup. Coffee. Straighten up and look around for the pot he boiled it in, for his stores. One of his pockets is sticking out like a white flag, and you check the woods as if the killer might be watching you. He's long gone, probably out of the county by now. You'll wire down the line to Shawano, tell Bart Cox to keep an eye out for tramps. Bart went to see the elephant with you and caught a minié ball in his arm at Bloody Run. The arm healed crooked, then went bad; Bart's still a crack shot with his other. He was a sergeant, and has less sympathy than you for these transients—brother soldiers be damned. But there are a lot of them out there, and your mother's missionary blood rises every time you think of them. They travel in twos often as not. Sad really, this one. Probably thought the man was his friend.

"God have mercy," you pray, then turn him over. No

blood on his filthy undershirt, no bullet holes, no bowie knife slipped between the ribs. His cuticles are purple, like he's dipped them in wine, and you wonder how long it's been. You'll have to talk to Doc, see what he says. You tuck the cap and the cup into the man's jacket, cross his arms over his belly, though they don't want to go. This is how they taught you in the army; it's easier on the back. You take him by the ankles, note the sliver-thin heels on his army-issue boots, the cracked leather.

There's no pretty way to do this, though you try to be careful. One day when your regiment was combing a meadow you broke a man's jaw for propping a dead Reb against a fencepost for a joke. If there's anything your jobs have taught you, it's to take death seriously, give it the same respect as love.

"It's all right," you find yourself saying to him. "We'll get you set proper, don't you fret." It's a bad habit, talking to the dead. Marta says you say more to them than the living, and while she's kidding, it just might be true. Sometimes in the cellar you hold long conversations with those you're working over, answering your own questions as you drain their veins, trying to find out what you really think about justice, destiny, Heaven. You wonder if you're getting too serious, growing old.

"Going soft," you say, and the man nods, his head jostling through a patch of wild aster, and you feel bad for joking with him. Spooked. It's just the uniform, the recognition that this could be you. By the time you get him to the hives, you're somber, and even the bees' mad industry doesn't bring a smile.

Meyer's still filling the bowl with clots of honey, the handle of the knife and his thin buckskin gloves dark with it. He has one of the twins pull his rig alongside the weeds and help you lift the dead man into the back. The springs squeak. The boy makes a face at the smell, tries not to look at the body. He seems incomplete without his brother, diminished. You don't know which one it is, Marcus or Thaddeus.

"Can we get something to cover him," you say, and not just from respect. You don't need folks in town gawking, making it their business. Since the mines shut down, gossip's been Friendship's biggest industry.

The boy comes back with a scrap of burlap and you fashion it over the body yourself. He climbs up on the seat. The smell of the horses is getting to you, making you think of mud, the way your stomach clenched when the Reb artillery whistled over.

"Take him straight to Doc Guterson's," you tell him.

"Yes, sir," he says, still afraid to look back, and teases the reins to set the team walking. The dead man bounces as they cross the yard, his heels banging the bed. The tin cup clatters, then slides off into the grass with a glint. Bitsi dashes through the timothy and scoops it up like a prize chick and gives it to you. The metal's already begun to warm. You tuck it in your pocket and head for your bicycle, leaning in the shade of the eaves. You want to get to town first, and you know boys when their father gives them the rig.

"Well?" Meyer calls over.

"Well, we'll find out."

"I don't know why they gotta come here, there's no work for them. Betcha I'll load up the gun with rock salt tonight, sure."

"Set your dogs out, that'll take care of them. Say, which one's that driving?"

"That's Thaddeus."

"Any problems with the Colony?"

"Nope, pretty quiet lately."

"That's good. You didn't touch him or move him around," you ask, sure that Meyer didn't, but it's your job to be suspicious, to think of things other people wouldn't.

"No, sir. I wanted nothing to do with him, you bet."

"All right," you say, and trade a last batch of pleasantries, thank Bitsi and set off.

The dust on the road has settled and you can see the ruts left by Meyer's rig. Barn swallows flit over the fields, hop post to post, calling. With every pump of your legs, the cup in your pocket worries your crotch. You don't like that Meyer called you sir. He's had money problems, that's why he's putting up honey to sell in town. He wouldn't kill a man, and he probably wouldn't rob one, but if there was something lying around he might just pick it up. That wouldn't have been true before his Alma died, but now he's got the twins and Bitsi all by himself, and that can make a man desperate. Last month in Shawano Oly Marsden lost two calves and the stationmaster shot him trying to rob the depot. Bart said he didn't even tie a mask on, just walked up to the window with a shotgun like it was his due. The stationmaster had a skeet pistol and put a hole through Oly's Adam's apple. So there was a man who drove his daughters to the parish dances, bleeding to death on the boards of the platform, the passengers from the noon train flowing around him like he was nothing. You don't like to think this way, so you stand up on the pedals and reach down and push the cup around so it doesn't fuss with you so much.

By law, the man was trespassing, so if Meyer did do something, he was in his rights. But that's a quibble, not really the spirit of the law. Meyer didn't kill him. Maybe he turned out his pockets, shook his pack out in the grass. Not honorable certainly, but criminal?

You shake your head to dismiss it. A man's dead, there's no room for these fine distinctions. Murder's always simple.

You mark the dust before you see the rig plodding along, the burlap thrown over him, Thaddeus still not looking back. You dip the brim of your hat, tuck your head down to keep the dust out of your eyes; it sticks to your lashes, powders your jacket. You dig hard to pass him, ignoring the horses, then give him a wave. In a few minutes you can't even see him behind you, only the fields, the treeline, the sky.

It's a perfect day, but you see the man sprawled across the fire, his one cheek dark with charcoal. You'll talk to Doc, he'll figure it out. You know it's best not to think too long on these things.

Karmanns started haying last week, and as you pass, thinking of the snap beans Marta promised this morning, you see a woman lying in the brilliant stubble. At first you think it's a fieldhand catching a nap, but she's wearing a shift, her hair bright as the dry ricks. She's facedown like your friend in the rig, and you slow and hop off and jump the ditch, thinking it can't be, two in the same day.

Before you even reach her, you panic and wonder if it's the work of one person, like those little girls Bart found in the smith's cistern. Now there was evil. Bart showed you the odd parts, the marks on their bodies, and while you prided yourself on having seen worse, this wasn't the war, these were just children. You helped Bart burn the smith's barn and then his house to the ground while the whole town watched, silent as mourners. It was a distraction; while you and Bart offered up his property, the smith was being whisked out the back door of the courthouse by the same marshal who took care of Eric Soderholm.

Tromping across the stubble, you wonder if the smith could have broken out of Mendota, if you'll have to wire Bart and tell him to bring the dogs. And it was such a pretty day too, you think, that quiet you like. Even now the trees are calm, riffling with the slightest breeze, then subsiding.

Closer, you can see she's a good-sized woman, older. She's from the city; you can tell by the gauzy chemise, the stockings, the high-buttoned shoes. Probably from the Colony. Occasionally they escape, go off on frolics in the saloons, and you have to corral them. You peer off over the field for a sign of Karmann or his boys, but there's no one, only a hawk riding the day's heat, spiraling high.

Her legs are scratched and bleeding, her stockings torn. You kneel by her feet for a better look. One line of blood's fresh, still wet, and when you touch a finger to it to make sure, she flips over and kicks your hand away.

You back up, automatically going for your Colt, but your hand never gets there because you're lost in watching her.

She jerks as if pitching a fit, thrashes her head side to side. Her neck is dirty, her hair all snarls, as if she's been living in the woods. You think of the Hermit's missing teeth, his curling fingernails, and pull your jacket back over the butt of your gun.

"Jesus Jesus Jesus," she moans. "Jesus Jesus Jesus."

"Ma'am!" you say, "Ma'am."

It takes a while, but she slows, lets her head drop. "Jesus I love you, Jesus I love you." It's like singing, pleading. Her eyes are squeezed so tight she's crying, but she sounds happy. "I love Jesus."

It's ecstasy, you see it each July when the revival comes through, their wagons painted with biblical scenes, bright as the circus. You've always thought it was fake, this rapture, a stage trick, a shill egging on the susceptible, filling the tent. You know the Lord as well as anyone, and there's no call for all that show. Could be she's been drinking.

"Ma'am," you say, and take her arm.

She lets you help her up, muttering, "Jesus my Lord and

savior," but when you try to lead her back to the road, she tears her wrist away and falls to the ground again. She writhes in the hay at your feet.

"Really, ma'am," you scold her. It's too hot for this, too buggy. You'll have to ride the handcar out the Nokes spur to the Colony now, see Chase.

You look back to the road, and there's Thaddeus, the rig stirring up dust. You wave both arms over your head, and he slows, the cloud closing over him.

The woman's gone quiet again, mumbling, eyes dull. She coughs and brings up something, a string hanging off her chin, and you step back, thinking she might be wild, mad like an animal. You've seen a diseased hog take a chunk out of a man's knee, the foam dripping green from its lips.

"I saw Jesus," she says, acknowledging you for the first time, and you think she's just sick, that there must be a simple reason behind all this. "I saw Jesus," she repeats. It's a question now, directed at you, a fact you seem to be disputing.

"I know you did," you say, because it's foolish to argue with crazy people. You offer her your hand and she takes it and you pull her up again.

"He was so beautiful. He's been waiting for me."

"For all of us," you say.

"Yes," she says. "How did you know?"

"I know something of him."

"Brother Chase says he saves all of us, the cleansed *and* the sick. Do you think that's true?" She stops and gapes at you as if you really might know.

"Of course," you say, "we're all saved," and steer her across the field. It's not a convenient lie either; you truly believe this. Otherwise you wouldn't have taken Reverend Toomey's place, preaching from his pulpit after the diocese called him back to Madison. Deacon Hansen, they call you Sunday, and then Monday you find they've given the milk-hand a black eye, that their youngest got himself cut up in a sporting house over in Shawano. It's all of a piece, you think; sheriff or deacon, you're trying to remind them of their best instincts, their better selves.

"All!" She laughs. "Ah, Brother, but you're not sick."

"No," you concede.

"It's easy to believe then."

You disagree with this but just nod. The whole idea of deathbed conversion strikes you as false, a sop for the dying. It's when you're happiest, sure of your own strength, that you need to bow down and talk with God. You wonder if that's lax or fanatic. You know Marta worries when you make too much of your faith, so you've taken to praying in your office when the cell's empty, the stone cold and hard on your knees. There's nothing desperate about it, just a comfort you rely on time to time, but you've given up trying to explain it. You can't, really. It's a feeling of almost knowing something, of being close to some grand yet utterly simple answer. But what that answer is, you don't know. It's easier to hide it, keep it private, which makes you ashamed. You don't trust people with secrets.

You walk the woman toward Thaddeus, who meets you halfway. He shies back from her, and, unfairly, you think

he's some squeamish for a farmboy. Bitsi didn't have any
trouble picking up that cup.

"Have you seen Jesus?" she asks him.

He looks to you, unsure what to say. "No, ma'am," he
says, tentative.

"He sees *you,*" she answers, as if the converse logically follows.

Thaddeus looks to you helplessly.

"He sees all of us," you say.

"That's right," the woman says, and lets loose another
hawking cough. She seems recovered, but that might be
temporary. You'll take her to Doc Guterson too.

The team is a pair of big Belgians, the kind that used to
draw the guns. They stand champing, veiny bellies wrig-
gling to toss off flies. The soldier's begun to stink with the
heat, and you can feel the past oozing up like mud. You
rearrange him under the burlap and lift the bike on, then
hop up to give the woman a hand in. Thaddeus is glad to
take the driver's seat again.

You shield the woman from the dead man, but she stares
at the burlap, rubs her nose with the back of a hand.
Thaddeus snaps the reins and the wheels grate over the
road. Your bike settles, the man's boots knock.

"In Heaven you forget everything," she says. "In Hell
they make you remember."

No, you think, it's the other way around. "Maybe so,"
you say.

"Everyone smells, even the saved. My Daniel smelled.
We laid hands on him but it was too late."

"Was he at the Colony?"

"Brother Chase said it's a sin, going against God's will. I think it is now, I do."

"Daniel was your husband," you ask, but she looks off over the fields. Weitzels are out haying, the smaller boy atop the wagon with a fork. Midsummer day, start to make hay. They're almost done, just one row of ricks left. They wave, and you know the whole town will be discussing this over supper, speculating on who the woman was, and what you had in the back of Old Meyer's rig. People will drop by tomorrow to see if she's in the cell.

"He takes the little ones first," the woman says, and you can't help but think of Amelia.

"I'm very sorry, ma'am," you say, thinking this might explain at least some of her behavior. If this really is the truth.

"Heaven's full of babies."

"It is."

She nods and coughs hard, and Thaddeus looks back an instant, as if he's forgotten you're there. From town comes the church bell tolling one. Doc should be getting up from his nap right about now, taking his collar off its stand, pinching the stays in place. He'll be able to help her.

The road turns along the river, under a row of weed trees. The heat makes the cicadas scream. As you rock through the dimness of Ender's bridge, you can hear children splashing and laughing below, the rafters holding an echo, pigeons lowing, and you nudge the man's boot back under the burlap. Into the sun again. The woman stares blankly at the wake of dust rising behind you. The ecstasy seems to have passed, and she looks spent, empty, old. The river's low, the flats cracked mud, the reeds rotting. The Belgians nicker at the smell.

Town's green though, cool. You take the last turn before Friendship proper, and the clapboard houses of your neighbors slide by, neat behind their picket fences, the oaks above a tunnel. You look up and the limbs pass overhead, dip as if blessing you. Flickers chirp, unseen. In the shade, the day seems easy again, but it's a trick. There's a man dead, a woman sick with grief.

Still, you think, snap beans for supper. You'll coax Marta into singing while you play the melodeon, and after Amelia's down, the two of you will read to each other from Mrs. Stowe until you reach the end of the chapter. One of you will trim the lamp, and in the dark Marta's hand will find yours. In bed you'll need the comforter, you'll snuggle down under it. That's the nice thing about living so far north; even in the heat of summer, the nights are cool. "Jacob," she'll say, and wish you sweet dreams. And lying there beside her, silently saying your prayers, you'll think, what a world this is, what luck you have, and you'll thank God, you'll let Him know how glad you are for everything—even the heat, the dust, the tears of this madwoman. And even you, then, will wonder how you have such hope, and marvel at how impossible it is to stop the heart from reaching out to the whole world—to all of your people here in Friendship, asleep under the summer moon—and alone in the dark you'll submit, give in to this great blessing, and think, yes, tomorrow will be a better day.

Maybe you are a fool. You remember what your mother used to say about Reverend Toomey: a holy fool is still a fool. It's not true, you think, not completely. Funny how you never agree to anything, keep that last piece of yourself back. Is it prudence or faithlessness—and does it matter to anyone but you?

The trees give way to Main Street, the sun hot on your hair. Fenton's out in his apron, dusting a rug over the hitching rail with a wire beater. You check the woman; she's muttering, shrugging, arguing with herself. Yancey Thigpen's mare is tied outside the livery, otherwise it's quiet, only the steam pulsing up from the mill, the distant drone of the saws. Thaddeus draws the team even with Doc's shingle. They stamp, their traces jingling, and you take the woman's arm.

"Thank you," she says, stepping down.

Across the street, Fenton's stopped thumping the rug. You motion for Thaddeus to get the door. First he wipes his boots on the edge of the sidewalk, and you're sorry for thinking poorly of him. The bell rings and you guide the woman inside.

Doc's parlor is empty and dark and smells of violets fresh from Irma's garden. She picked out the furniture in Chicago, and no one wants to sit on it. Even the city woman's impressed, inspecting the flocked wallpaper, the golden innards of the clock in its bell jar.

"Hello," you ask.

"Be a minute," Doc calls from the back, behind the curtain. He splashes water in a basin, bangs a cupboard shut.

"It's me," you call. "I brought company."

He flings the curtain aside like a magician. He's just gotten up, small and dapper in his pin-striped suit and stiff boiled shirt, hair parted in the middle and brilliantined, mustache waxed. People say he's taken to fancy ways since marrying, but that's jealousy. Irma's from Milwaukee, a teacher at the state normal school, and a few families here with prettier daughters are still bitter. And he's always been fastidious; he orders his shoes through the mail, buys his shirts ten at a time.

"Oh my dear," he says, noticing the woman, and goes over to her. She's bigger than he is. "We're not doing so well, are we?"

"Careful there," you say, and tell him how you found her.

"Right," he says, "I see," more interested in her neck. "I don't think that's going to be a problem, do you?" he asks her.

"No," she says absently, all the fight gone out of her. "Thank you."

He tips her chin up to feel along her jaw, and you notice a bandage on his hand.

You ask.

"Just clumsy," he shrugs. He gives Thaddeus a nod. The boy returns it, his hat in both hands, shy, polite. "Why don't you bring the other fellow in? This may take a bit."

Thaddeus waits for you to move, and again you're impatient with him.

You forgot how hot it was, how bright. Fenton's gone back inside, Yancey's mare flinging her tail to drive off flies. You try to keep the burlap over the soldier, drag him across the back of the wagon like a sack, get him under the armpits. The boy just stands there.

"Lend a hand there, if you would," you say, not too hard, and Thaddeus takes his ankles.

You walk backward, your heels searching for the edge of the sidewalk, the step up. You're glad he's not a fat one. You remember wrestling Mrs. Goetz onto the table in the cellar, turning your knee and cursing her, then that night praying for patience. What was it you said last week in your sermon—even the meanest work is a form of praise? No wonder Marta worries you'll end up in the Colony, dancing jaybird naked in the woods, a candle in each hand.

You shoulder the door open and the bell tinkles.

"Hold on," Doc calls, and bursts through the curtain with his shirtsleeves rolled. "Put him down."

"Here?"

"Put him down," he orders, almost scolding, and before you can give him a look, he says it again. "On the floor. Now."

"What is it?" you ask, but he's pulled the burlap off and kneels by the man's face—the sunken eyes and greening skin. He leans in close as a lover, slips a hand between the man's teeth and pulls down his jaw.

"That lamp," he says, pointing, and you give it to him. He sets the glass chimney aside and lights it, holds it over the man's face. Flecks of wheat stick in his whiskers. Doc's fingers rummage around in his mouth, under his tongue, as if searching for a hidden jewel. Beside you, Thaddeus is transfixed.

Doc stands up and fits the lamp back together. "Take him next door and try not to touch him too much."

"What is it?"

"Just take him down the cellar for now. I'll talk to you when I get her settled."

"She acting up?"

"You could say that. Just get him down, will you? And make sure and wash up good, both of you."

"Okay," you say, but hesitant, to let him know he's being strange.

You rearrange the burlap, pick the soldier up and walk backwards again, brushing the jamb, tottering down the walk one door to your place. It's open, and as you maneuver through, you see Fenton over the boy's shoulder, peering from his door.

Thaddeus looks around your office at the empty cell, the rifles locked to the wall, the old posters. What an adventure he's having; how jealous Marcus will be. And now you're taking him down to a room the boys of Friendship whisper about, the boldest professing intimate knowledge around dying campfires.

There's nothing to see—the clay walls, the table with its gutter draining into a pail, a few casks of fluid, a miter by a stack of cured cedar cut to the three usual lengths. Your tools hang neatly on the rough beams, polished and gleaming in the lamplight. To him it must seem ghoulish, fantastic as Ali Baba's cave. You want to tell him it's a job, and not simply a necessary one, but a last opportunity to care for another person, to serve their family.

You get the soldier onto the table. If it were just you, you'd strap him in and turn the crank so the whole thing would tilt, but the boy's seen enough for one day. You thank him and he thumps up the stairs.

"It's cold down there," he says, washing over the basin.

"Stays the same the year round." It's an old trick, you want to tell him. A hundred years ago the French used it to summer their furs. In the winter you store Friendship's dead down there, their coffins waiting for the ground to thaw out. You want to tell him about the conversations they have, the arguments over things long forgotten. You want to impress on him how many stories everyone has within them, how much each death diminishes Friendship, especially with the young people leaving. But again, he's done enough. And he's young, you don't expect him to understand. Outside, he lifts your bike over the side of the rig, and you thank him once more before he starts off.

Yancey's mare is gone, but John Cole's sorrel and buckboard are hitched at Fenton's. You slip into Doc's as if for an afternoon chat.

The parlor's empty, in back the sound of water sloshing.

"That you, Jacob?" he calls, and you answer. "I'll just be a minute."

You slap the dust off your bottom before sitting on Irma's love seat. You wonder what Doc saw. Usually he'll take you into his examining room and go over the littlest detail with you, as if you're a student. Maybe it was starvation, and he was too busy with the woman. You don't believe it, the way the man pitched into the fire. When soldiers go hungry too long, they liberate food. And it's not like Doc to boss you around. Make sure and wash up good, he said. This is the hard part of being a constable: when it comes to Friendship, you don't like mysteries. You worry too much. It's like Amelia's colic; you want to be sure it's normal, that in the morning you won't find her blue and motionless in her crib.

Doc comes in with his jacket on, his bandage missing. He takes a seat behind his desk without looking at you, leans back and crosses his legs—a city thing. He's frowning, going over something in his mind, and you know not to interrupt.

"You say the fellow's pockets were turned out," he asks.

"Probably his traveling companion. Why, what is it?"

"If I'm right," he says, "diphtheria."

"Diphtheria," you echo, trying it out in your mouth. Endeavor went through an epidemic a few years ago, took half the town. And Montello had that typhus that went through the tannery there, killed all those women. You'll have to enforce quarantine, burn the dead's possessions. But of the disease itself you're mostly ignorant. It kills, that's enough.

"Don't bother dressing him out," Doc says. "Just get him in the ground. And be damned careful how you handle him."

"Right."

The two of you sit there a minute in the cool room, pondering what this means to Friendship. Your thoughts refuse to connect, run together like the cicadas outside, screaming in the trees.

"Guess I better wire down the line and let Bart know," you say, but it's a question. You're hoping Doc will back off and say he could be mistaken, that the woman's symptoms could be anything. Diphtheria kills quick, that's the one thing you know. You think of what the woman said—He takes the little ones first.

"Yep," Doc says, half-distracted, and sighs, an admission of failure. "I guess you'd better."

2

"We can leave," Marta says for the fifth time tonight. You're in bed, under the comforter, but no one's going to sleep. "We'll take what we need and go to Aunt Bette's."

"We can't," you whisper. You're nose to nose, inches apart, one thigh clamped between her knees. "I can't. You know that."

"I know."

She's so disappointed it makes you want to give in, and she knows this. All night she's apologized for making you feel it's your fault, but it is, and she has, so there's no point. You don't know how to argue; it's a weakness in you. After the war, you lost the will to fight, the interest in getting your way in little things. Your strategy is to make her happy, keep the peace—at worst, retreat, take the blame. But there's no argument here. Your duty seems plain. You hold her closer, smell the warmth of her neck, the taste of the day's work on her—the tang of salt pork caught in her hair. Her breasts are tender; they leak when Amelia cries.

"Jacob, if I took her to Bette's. For a visit."

"How would that look?"

"I don't care how it looks."

"You don't?" you ask, bold, because you know Marta's not selfish, that she loves Friendship as much as you do.

"I do," she concedes. "But what am I supposed to do—stay in the house all day while you go out? And if you should get it, what then?"

You tell her you know how to handle the dead, that once the disease spreads, you'll need her even more, but you picture the soldier this afternoon, how you forced his stiff arms into the box and slid the lid shut, banged the nails home with three even strokes. You tell her Doc knows what he's doing; he got Amelia through the croup, didn't he? In the dark, she sighs, unmoved, and you realize your argument is calm and logical where hers is spurred by a mother's fear. You realize you've entirely mistaken the issue you're debating.

"You can go if you want. I'll say it's a visit."

"No," she says, bitter, even though she's won. "We'll stay."

You part, roll over so you're both facing away, but you turn and fit your knees behind hers. She takes your hand and bites one knuckle in forgiveness.

"I'll be careful," you reassure her. "I'll be with Doc."

"I know," she says, but unconvinced, and shifts again, her

hair tickling your forehead. This debate could go on indefinitely, rage silently while you rearrange yourselves, plump the pillows. Finally a long stretch of quiet, her breathing drawn and soft, and then from the nursery comes a hiccup and a siren of a cry as Amelia realizes she's awake. Marta sighs and folds the comforter aside, staggers to the rocker to calm her. You wait in the dark, listening to them creak, then Amelia cooing, Marta's song about the bear who ate too many blueberry pies.

You don't remember falling asleep, or your dreams, though you know they were vivid, disturbing—a house with too many doors, tilting like a ship in high seas. You wake suddenly to daylight, the smell of frying butter. The blinds are up, but Marta's closed the door, her robe hung from the peg. Outside it's brilliant, another perfect day, and you try to hold off thoughts of the coffin you buried in the weedy edge of the churchyard, the woman Doc has locked in his office.

It breeds in the heat, he said.

You lie there and watch the light turning the leaves transparent. It seems wrong that this can kill. Rain seems more appropriate, long gray days, cold.

There's no time to philosophize. You pitch out of bed and haul on some clean dungarees, pour an inch of water in the basin and wash your face. Take a second in the mirror to trim your beard with Marta's sewing scissors, tilting your chin until you achieve the exact fashion the captain of your regiment wore. Buttoning up a clean shirt, you think you're just as fastidious as Doc in your own way. But that too has to do with responsibility. An officer provides his men a model of cleanliness, order, decorum, and a town, like an army, looks to its leaders. You quiz your neat twin in the glass. Do you really believe this or are you just hoping? It's like you to be steadfast when panic would serve you better.

Marta peeks in the door and says, "Breakfast."

"Why didn't you wake me up?"

"You were tired."

You thank her, hoping last night's business is over, knowing it isn't.

Open the door and you can smell corncakes and sausage. It's strategic—all week it's been oatmeal—and you try to conjure your arguments, the line you need to cleave to.

Amelia hangs on Marta's ankles at the stove. Marta placates her with the straw dolly; Amelia gnaws on its head. Coffee's on the table, too hot. The sausage pops in the skillet. Marta has her back to you, and you watch her elbow digging the cakes up, flipping them. She must know it's too late to change things. And it's the right decision, it's the Christian thing to do.

She lays the plate in front of you and stands back to gauge your pleasure in her work. The butter runs. They're rich, the edges crisp, middles still doughy. You nod with your mouth full, toss back a burning slug of coffee to help it down. Maybe the woman's an isolated case, the soldier her lover, the woods their nightly rendezvous. It's your fear of disappointing Marta that makes you cast about like this.

You smile at her and pin a sausage with the side of your fork until the skin splits, spear it and cram in another bite. Satisfied, she unties the apron and sits beside you.

"Stopping by Doc's first?" she asks.

It takes you a minute to swallow, and then it goes down hard. "He's the boss on this one. Maybe she's better today."

"Let's hope."

"You never know with these things," you say, and it could be true, couldn't it?

"Have you talked with Bart at all?"

"I wired him yesterday."

"What did he say?"

"He said, 'Good luck.' "

You look down and all you've got left is a nub of sausage, a sodden wedge of corncake. You've wolfed it; it happens when you're nervous or thinking too hard.

"More?" Marta says.

"No thank you. Guess my stomach's gotten used to just oatmeal."

"I thought you'd want something stronger today."

"I did," you say, but just to agree with her. It puzzles you that she's given up so easily. If she left on the morning stage, she could be at Bette's before sundown. You finish and she takes the plate, walks over to the stove where she's got a kettle going. She ties her apron on again, clanks the dishes into a tin tub and pours the hot water over them, sets to work as if this is just another day. She's calmer than you, and you think it's her faith you aspire to, her unswerving belief that attracted you to her, not her long hands or her hair, the way her upper lip flattens in the middle, turns suddenly lush. Tonight maybe you'll take her out by the garden and sing to her.

Amelia latches on to your boot, her heavy head resting on the toe, and you pick her up, your hand steadying her warm, pudgy neck. Her eyes light dreamily on yours and she coos. You coo back, make a face and watch hers change, unsure.

"Going out the Colony?" Marta asks from the tub.

"To see Chase. I imagine so."

"You be careful out there. That whole place could be diseased the way they live."

"I'll keep my distance."

The church bell tolls seven-thirty, and you gulp your coffee. If the soldier was from town, at daybreak Cyril Lemke, the sexton, would ring the bell one time for every year of his life, but he's an outsider, and the sun comes up quiet. The coffee's strong. You want a second cup, but it's a luxury you can't afford today. You set Amelia down and she cries, weeps, shrieks. Marta croons over her shoulder, trying to soothe her. It's the hard part of the morning, leaving. Marta shrugs; it's not your fault. Babies cry.

You head for the silence of the bedroom and grab your gun belt from its shelf and buckle it on, slip the Colt from its holster and check the cylinder, make sure all six are there. You've never needed them—or only against that mad hog (who took all six before pitching over)—but people expect you to be handy with a gun, and you are. Saturdays you practice out by the Hermit's lake—the surface ringed green with scum—picking skinny patent-medicine bottles off a log. Carl Soderholm down at the apothecary saves them for you. It's an exercise you read about in a Wild West dime novel, but it seems to work. Last Saturday you were five for six, and only missed the one because the freight blew its whistle just as you were squeezing the last shot off. If you had to shoot a cigarette out of someone's mouth like in the book, you could probably do it in four or five tries.

In the kitchen, Amelia's finally stopped crying, her head against Marta's chest. Marta sways in place, shifting hip to hip. Their hair is precisely the same shade, and their eyes; there's no trace of you in Amelia's face, and sometimes you wonder if they need you at all, if you're really a part of them. It's fleeting, this worry, and turns quickly into wonder at how lucky you are. Certainly you're unworthy of such love.

You kiss Marta on the forehead, taste the soap on her skin. "You can take her and go."

"We'll be fine," she says, dismissing the idea with a wave. "You're the one who needs to be careful."

"I will."

"And stop in at Fenton's for me? He'll know what I want."

"I will."

You kiss her again, and then you're past her, almost out of the house, but at the door you stop, as if to give her one last chance.

"Go," she says, laughing at you. "I was being a silly chicken."

Her smile more than forgives you. She's pleased that you're doing the right thing. She believes in you. It's why she loves you—that you care about this town, that she can be sure you'll do what's best for everyone. But once you close the door and walk out into the dusty street, the smile you gave her slips from your face, and you wish she'd fought harder, that she'd stopped you. Because you know you're wrong.

You ride your bike to town. It's already hot, the shadows of oaks sharp on the road, dust clinging to the bright fireweed. Before the trees give way to the shadeless plain of Main Street, you hear a rig rattling behind you, a team puffing along. You move right to let them through, and as they appear over your shoulder, you see it's Chase with his women in the bed of the wagon, sitting on hay bales. His clothes are the same as yours—a boiled shirt and a black cravat, dungarees and boots—but they're new and sit on him like a costume. City money, everyone says, spitting it like a curse.

"Deacon," he calls, and waves, neighborly, and you nod. He's a big man, built solid as a Canuck logger, with the same bluff charm. In the army, you were glad to serve under men like him; it was the little drunkards that got their regiments killed.

The women mark you and smile. Some of the newer ones still wear their city clothes, but the few you recognize sport a simple uniform—a white blouse and a black shift, their hair pinned up in caps like Mennonites. There are always new ones coming in. It's said some of them don't have men, which leads to murkier speculations you want no part of. Their dust covers you, then clears.

It's only Tuesday, you think. They do their shopping Wednesday, regular, the women fanning out through town, paying cash, aggressively pleasant. Maybe it's not remarkable, but you've schooled yourself in the way Friendship operates. You know when the smallest thing is out of place, and today you're on guard.

When you reach Main Street, your suspicion proves true. Chase's empty rig is parked in front of Doc's, the team tied up so they can't dip at the trough. They see you and stamp impatiently, as if—like blueticks—they can smell the history of your fear. You lean your bike against the rail and climb the sidewalk, prop your door wide with the spittoon to let everyone know you're open. The cell's empty, the rifles locked to the wall. You conduct this inventory out of habit rather than any true necessity. Your desk is clean, yesterday neatly marked off on the wall calendar. The order soothes you, but just for an instant. It's going to be a busy day—when all you really want to do is bike down the river road and take the handcar out west along the Montello line, maybe hike up on top of Cobb's tunnel and soak in the view, the county spread around you like a map.

Not today. You double-check the gun rack, then head next door, wondering how you defend yourself against sickness.

In the parlor, Chase towers over Doc. He seems far too large, and confused—like a bear wandered into a shop, strangely out of place. Doc fusses with a brass paperweight, sliding the milled disk over his blotter like a pawn. Chase turns away, paces, rubbing one eyebrow as if thinking. You've interrupted them.

Doc seems relieved. "I've been telling Reverend Chase of the possible consequences of the disease."

"I'm aware of the consequences," Chase says, trying to be polite. "We're prepared to take care of her. We have three certified nurses among us."

"No doctor."

"No."

"And what sort of quarantine would you enforce?"

"Whatever you suggest."

"Total," Doc says.

"Fine," Chase says, as if he's gotten the short end of the bargain but is still glad to have it settled. He wants to be civil just as much as Doc. "Can I see her now?"

"I'm not suggesting it for this case but for the next one that crops up. I'd like to keep Miss Flynn here. She needs a doctor."

"For how long?"

"A day. Two. However long she lasts."

He delivers this so quickly that you wonder if it's deliberately mean. The news makes you look at Chase. For an instant, standing in profile by Irma's striped wallpaper, head bent, he seems heavy, defeated, but then, with effort, he straightens up and puts on a pained smile. "If there's nothing to be done, can't we have her home?"

"Too contagious, I'm afraid," Doc says, genuinely sorry.

"I understand."

For a moment the parlor's silent except for the clock ticking in its bell jar, and you can hear the birds outside, a gust of air rustling the trees like a wave, then subsiding, giving way to cicadas. You wonder why you're trapped in this room with these two. You have nothing to say, other than you're sorry.

You do. It doesn't seem enough, but Chase thanks you anyway.

"If I could see her," he asks, and from the tone it's clear Doc could say no and he wouldn't argue. You're not surprised he's reasonable, willing to cede his authority. Grief breaks down all but the crazy; it's a secret of your profession, one people don't want to know. Another secret you've just found out: Chase is sane. The stories people tell make him out to be a tyrant, wild-eyed, and it's heartening to see they're untrue. He's like Doc, you think—he's like you—just trying to do the best for his flock.

"I can let you visit with her briefly, but I don't want you getting too close." Doc waits for Chase to agree to this before he gets up and searches his middle drawer for a key.

You follow them through the curtain and down the hall, past the tasteful landscapes and still lifes Irma bought in Milwaukee. You expect Chase is used to such elegance, or perhaps he's too busy to comment on it, his mind elsewhere, preoccupied. You notice you're only thinking of Irma's touches because you don't want to picture the woman, that you'd be happier not seeing her at all.

Miss Flynn, he called her. You think of Mrs. Goetz tumbling from the pew, her head grazing the hassock, saved from the cool floor by her neighbor's foot. You knelt down and watched her go, her lips trying to fit around one final word. It's hard to lose anyone, especially when your flock's small to begin with.

Doc bends to jiggle the key in, and the bolt clacks back.

"I don't want you to touch her," he warns Chase.

"I understand."

Doc leads him in. You linger on the Persian runner, wondering again what you're supposed to do. That fascinating green summer light you love is filtering through the window at the end of the hall, throwing a winking pattern of shadows across the floor.

"Merciful Jesus," Chase says, and you hear a thump, as if he's fallen.

He's on his knees by her bedside, and, not really wanting to, you see her.

She's like the soldier, her eyes sunken in violet pits, cheeks creased and hollow. Her pupils move but she doesn't register any of you; they flit as if tracking a fly. Doc has wrapped a mint plaster about her neck. She wheezes with every breath, her lips stained as if she's been drinking wine. On the nightstand sits a basin of water tinged pink with blood, a stack of folded washcloths. Chase bends his head and mutters over his clenched hands, and you find the scene has drawn you into the room.

You stand beside Doc, watching Chase pray, feeling the

urge yourself, and when he reaches for her there's nothing either of you can do. He leans his head down and presses the back of her hand to his lips. When he lays it back in place, you see the cuticles are purple, the blood settling as if she's already dead.

"That was very dangerous," Doc says in the parlor.

"I'm sorry," Chase says, dabbing his eyes with a handkerchief. He sits on the love seat, hanging his head. He's been teary intermittently, overwhelmed by the sight of her. He's told you how Lydia Flynn's family threw her out after she lost her factory job, how she'd become a hard woman and how he'd found her one evening selling herself in the Milwaukee train station. Her hands were black from the soot of the girders. Years ago, he says, and you wonder how that can be; he looks no older than forty. You think of the rumors about the women of the Colony. Maybe there's some truth to them. It only makes you like Chase more, his ministering to the fallen. Or is that sentimental?

The church bell strikes nine, and Chase looks up. "I better be going." He frowns and composes himself, pockets the hanky and stands. "They'll be waiting on me."

He's right. Outside, the women are piled into the back of the wagon with their sacks and bags and boxes, talking. They've done a week's shopping in less than twenty minutes. Their efficiency frightens Marta; she likens them to ants—mindless, dutiful. As Chase climbs on, they go through their purses, fishing up bills and handfuls of change. The woman closest to him collects everything and presents it to him. He stands to fit it into his wallet, then sits and takes the reins. You can see the line where the team's sweat has dried, the dark sheen where their hair has absorbed it. The smell makes you take a step back.

"I'll be by tomorrow morning," he tells Doc. "If anything should happen, I'd be grateful if you'd send word."

"I can take care of that," you say, pleased to finally be of some help.

"I'm obliged," Chase says, and before he flicks the reins, he reaches down and shakes first Doc's hand and then yours. Together, you watch them off.

"Man's an idiot," Doc says inside.

"Seemed genuine to me," you say, and you're surprised to find yourself defending him.

"I'm not saying that," Doc says. "He can bawl all he wants. I just got through telling him not to touch her, and what does he do?"

"It's only natural."

Doc harrumphs. He examines his palm, glaring at the cut.

"How is it?"

"Better," he says, and turns it over, moves the paperweight, stewing.

"You think he did it just to get your goat."

"Could be. Or some other reason. You never know with those types."

You want to challenge him, ask him exactly what he means by *those types,* but the argument's old, there's no point. You already know. He means people who let their faith take the place of their reason, people who believe this world is just a prelude to another, more glorious life. He means people like you.

The afternoon goes slowly. Even inside the air is thick and smells of dust. You sit at your desk, dealing hands of red dog to imaginary gamblers. A wood bee worries the frame of the cell's one window. You think of walking over to the old depot to ask Harlow Orton to wire Bart and ask if he's seen your tramp. You're betting he hasn't. It's uncharitable, but you can't shake the feeling that Meyer turned out the dead man's pockets. Men get desperate and drift into sin. You fold a pair of threes and discover you would've won. Shuffle, deal. At home Marta's probably worried about you. Maybe you'll take a ride over. But you won't. You're supposed to be here, so you are.

You're here when Millie Sullivan rolls up in her buckboard. She doesn't even hop off.

"It's Clytie," she says, meaning their milk cow's out again. Clytie's breachy, and as strayward it's your job to fetch her back. You do this for Millie once a week, telling her to mend the fence or you'll fine her, though she knows you won't. It's just her and Elsa out on the Endeavor Road, two widow ladies who married brothers. There's no blood between them but they fight like family. The last time you were called out because Elsa had stuck a fork an inch into Millie's arm—over what you're not sure. With Elsa it could be anything; she thinks demons live in the woods and doesn't leave the house. She accuses Millie of coveting her money, of slowly poisoning her. There are rumors of a bag in a mattress, jars full of silver dollars lining the shelves of the root cellar. They're untrue, just the usual box-social claptrap. The only thing they own is Clytie, and they can't even keep ahold of her.

"I'll come get her," you say, but Millie's not listening. She's already turning the buckboard around in the middle of Main Street. You toe the spittoon aside and close your door, then hop on your bike. The way she babies her team you'll beat her there.

The cranberry bogs west of town are parched, burned brown. Dragonflies slice by, wings shimmering. It's good to be moving, and you stand up on the pedals and race a scarlet tanager, winning when he lights on a fencepost, but even as you slow, letting the breeze cool you, you know you're trying not to think of the soldier, of the awful possibilities. Marta always scolds you for your ability to ignore the least thing painful, your sudden, incongruous bursts of cheer. Now you think she's right. Sometimes you envy the Hermit's life, the simplicity of speaking only to ducks, water, sky. What a comfort it must be not to care, to be ignorant of your neighbor's worries. Insane, true, but a relief.

The house looks deserted when you ride up, as it always does. Out front the roses are overgrown, twining up the porch; the grass is thigh-high and yellow from the sun, Queen Anne's lace mixed in. You'll have to talk to Fred Lembeck, convince him to take a scythe to the yard. You peer up at Elsa's window, the curtains hanging limp. She must be in bed. Must be hot up there under that tin roof. Still, better being shut up in an invalid room than the state hospital. You went to Mendota once, taking an escaped patient, a woman with a mania for breaking windows. You still remember the screaming, how it echoed off the stone—the sores on the woman's ankles, the bone showing through. Millie's right to keep her here.

You lean your bike against the shady side of the porch, then walk around back past the grape arbor and inspect the fence.

The whole length of it is busted up, posts knocked cock-eyed, rails' edges splintered and skinned down to the blond heart of the wood. Looks like someone took a sledge to it, or a bunch of someones. The Ramsay boys, you think, remembering last Halloween when they swabbed the fence with creosote and set it on fire. One post is knocked clean over, the hole busy with ants. What did they use? You don't see any sledge marks. There's a tuft of something caught on one of the rails. Black hair, short like a dog's. Farther down there's another clump, and a splash of blood. It's sad, but you wouldn't put it past the Ramsays to torture the poor beast. You can see her hoofprints on the road, and on the far side a snapped sapling where she shouldered into the woods.

Millie rattles up in the buckboard, and you head back to the house, winding between Clytie's hardening pies. Grasshoppers pop. Their kitchen garden is withered, the squash tiny and rotting on the vine. You look to the sky hopefully; it's so clear it's nearly white, the sun directly overhead. You know it rained a few weeks ago, but you can't picture it out here—the drops making the leaves nod, the barrel frothing to the top, overflowing.

"How's your well holding out?" you ask Millie.

"I'm careful with it," she says, as if you've accused her. You'll never get used to her defensiveness, her refusal to see you as a friend. You're the only one who comes out here, maybe the only person she sees all week. You'd want to talk, catch up on gossip; you'd invite yourself in, fix a little tea-cake the way Mrs. Paulsen does, hobnob in the parlor.

"She gone off through there," Millie points.

"I'll find her."

"Make sure and lock her in the stall when you're done," she says, and creaks up the porch stairs, a hand on the peel-ing railing. Her curtness is nothing new, but you're always hopeful, always ready to step into people's lives. It's the best part of being a deacon, pastoral care. Just seeing how people get along day to day is enough to balance out the hard truths of your other jobs. It's all one, you like to say, but don't lie, you have your favorites.

This isn't one of them. Clytie reminds you of those horses you owe your life to, the ones your regiment ate raw from the inside out those long weeks, sleeping between their empty ribs while the Reb shells whined all night. Clytie makes you think of the nameless friends you had to load into wagons like sides of meat, of how small you are, how weak. You're more comfortable with animals smaller than you—dogs and cats, animals capable of showing love—and this is a failing, you think. You need to embrace all creation, not just the easy parts.

You drape your jacket over a post, strip the top of the sapling for a switch and start off into the woods. The track's clear—grass crushed under hooves, the bent heads of ferns. It's cooler in the shade, moss spotting the sides of the trees, beds of trillium. Bark torn off, another clump of hair. You try not to brush up against anything; you're wearing a new shirt, and Marta's tired of you ruining them.

On one trunk you find a swipe of blood, and again you think of the Ramsays, their history with slingshots, the windows you've made their mother pay for. You imagine Clytie missing an eye, weeping runnels of blood. Children aren't cruel, just curious. Like scientists, they just want to see how things work, what might happen.

There's blood on the grass, splashed across the face of a daisy. You stop to listen, thinking she might be close. Birds chirping, the rustle of a chipmunk. Frog lunk. Nothing.

You follow the drips along a stony wash, across an orange bed of pine needles. The trail passes an old campfire circle, a ring of stones, and you think of your tramp. It's tinder back here, logs rotted to dry mush. Any other summer this would be marsh, the black mud sucking at your boots. Even the ferns are yellow. A stray ember from the late freight and the whole woods could go up.

More blood. Dark puddles of it in the dust, bright swatches on leafy weeds. Flies take a last taste before lifting into the air. The Ramsays must have cut her throat. Again, it reminds you of Kentucky, searching for your gut-shot buddies, following the same livid trails. You steer clear of the blood, saving your pants. You whip the switch and it sings.

Ahead, hidden by a little hillock, there's a cracking of sticks.

Stop. Crows scolding in the trees. A single, sweeter chirp. Then the cracking again, snapping, brush thrashing.

It's her, and without thinking, before you even see her, you circle around to your left, trying to get behind her so you can drive her back toward the road. Keep to the soft, sweet pine duff, try to be quiet. Like war, half of this job is tactics. The thrashing grows louder, as if she's rolling around or caught in a snare. Closer, you can hear her wet snorts—she's been running. You crouch down; you don't want to spook her, send her charging off again. Doc's going to need you in town. You wonder how the woman from the Colony's doing. You've got better things to do than clean up the Ramsays' mischief.

You reach the lip of the hillock. You're so close you can smell her, the rich musk of dung. Her breathing's slowed now, wheezing like a bellows. She's not young, Clytie. It makes you think of Doc, how someday you'll have to tend to him, but you shrug it off before you finish the thought, before you can picture it.

You'll have to trim his mustache, clip the stray nose hairs. Be as neat as he is.

The brush crackles, and you swear you hear her grunt, like a man lifting something heavy. Then a dull thud and a rustle of branches. Gasps, more snorting.

"All right," you say, and stand, switch in hand, as if she might surrender to weapons.

She doesn't turn to you. They've beaten her about the head. Her muzzle's foamy with blood, a beard of bubbles dripping from her lips. There's blood on the grass all around her. She's shaky on her legs, she's fouled herself. Her eyes are locked on a tree a few feet in front of her; it's splintered, the bark chopped and dark with blood.

"Ho!" you cry, but she pays no attention. "Ho, Clytie!"

She rears, then drives forward, lunges at the trunk. She tucks her head down and rams it.

The collision sounds like a dull ax striking, echoes through the empty woods. The leaves shake; a few fall. Her rear swings around and she twists, falling sideways onto a patch of grass.

She tries to get up but one leg's caught underneath her. She lifts it, and it's in two pieces. The hoof dangles below the knee like a broken fishing pole. She walks on it, stumbling, crushes it so the bone drives through. She limps back to take another run at the tree, stands there tilted, the skin of the leg a black rag, snorting, her nostrils blowing bubbles of blood.

Mad then. Not the Ramsays. And you think of the woman in the field, how some form of madness must accompany the sickness. Is that diphtheria? You'll have to ask Doc.

Clytie hawks froth, but this isn't Clytie. Now you wish it *was* the Ramsays. You drop the switch. You unsnap your holster and check the cylinder. You've got to get a little closer, get a clean shot at the heart. The head's messy, you've learned that at least twice in your life.

Clytie pants, resting for the next charge. If she would just fall over, you think, but you know she won't. The tree's just as smashed up as the fence.

"Ho!" you call, and step out of the brush.

She doesn't turn, and you walk straight for her, the gun out in front of you like a divining rod. You cock the hammer, feel the trigger dig into your finger. Her head is huge, the skin gashed and livid. Her eye rolls, picking you up. You see her as a massive deer, her heart lodged just below the shoulder. You let off three shots, and she's still looking at you, her giant eye taking you in, accusing.

You have three more. You hope and hope, there in the bright clearing, the sun cutting through to settle hot on the back of your hand, but she stands there breathing, stunned, unsure who you are.

You raise the barrel, sight on her eye, the black dot a target. A breeze floats through and the shadows dance across her face. Just one shot. You don't feel it now, but later you know you'll see this as merciful. Now you're not so sure. Why agonize? It's a responsibility, not a choice. But you do. More for yourself, you think; this hesitation's a luxury in the face of another's pain. You shrug the thought off, still clinging to some dream of innocence, blamelessness, even as you release it. You turn back to this world. You do what's right.

3

Days go by, and nothing. Town's quiet, the middle of the week a hammock you sink into. The county's busy with threshing. Nobody on the road, only the wail of the late freight. Stones clunk in your spokes. You pour kerosene on Clytie, recite a few well-chosen lines and touch a spunk to her, and the smoke rolls up through the birches, the leaves spinning silver.

You talk with Doc about a quarantine, but he doesn't want to chance a panic. The woman from the Colony worsens; her mumbling drifts in the hall, seeps through the curtain into the dim parlor. Lydia Flynn, Doc has to prompt you. You can't remember her name, only her rolling eyes, her glazed, crazy speech. Chase comes every morning, bringing biscuits and casseroles she can't eat. Doc won't let him in the room, so he sits with you, worried as a new father, his hat in his lap.

Summer days long as the old post road and twice as dry. At lunch you go home and visit Marta. You sweep the jail, keep the cellar neat. You sit at your desk and deal losing hands to yourself, go out on the sidewalk and squint into the afternoon. Take your bike and fly between the high fields. Hawks, sun, blue.

Worry rolls inside you like a wheel. What's the connection between Clytie and the tramp? The woman from the Colony? How long till it hits town? Or will it pass by, suddenly veer into the fields like a twister?

Marta stays inside all day. "Everyone else is out," she argues, pointing to the window, the oak-shaded street. You don't fight, it's just a complaint she wants you to register.

"I know," you say, but don't explain, take a bite of pie.

Neither does she ask you to, your combined silence fearful, tinged with guilt. Shouldn't you tell everyone what's coming? You conjure Doc, the idea of needless panic, hysteria. It'll come soon enough.

At night Marta takes you to her, and in the morning Amelia clutches your pantleg, rides your knee, giggling. A paper man shows up and glues a shaky masterpiece to the side of Ender's bridge—leering clowns and slope-browed elephants; the Ringling Brothers are coming in two weeks. The *County Record* expects the weather to turn in time to save tomato season. Marta holds the door and waves goodbye; you've told her to lock it behind you, but when she does it's a loss, a betrayal of your faith. Outside, riding to town, you marvel at the bounty of the trees, the hills, the endless invention set before you, but inside the jail, your boots crossed on the desk, you know you're just waiting.

You go to Doc, hoping he can soothe you, tell you Friendship's lucky, that you've dodged it this time. His parlor's dark, cool as a fruit cellar.

"Wait and see," he says. "Wait and see."

You do. You tick the hours off on your railroad watch, then pump the handcar out to Cobb's tunnel, climb the winding path and stand on top facing west, the green humps of hills running to a hazy infinity. The late freight's on time, the plume a gray exclamation in the distance, so far off you can't hear it. Then the chuffing, the throaty steam. A long one, lots of hoppers. Wheat. You follow it until it's under you, the hill shaking as it plunges through the tunnel, the cloud passing over you like a warm rain. And then it's gone, hissing in the distance, finally quiet, just a shadow moving toward town and the horizon, down the line to Shawano. You wonder if Bart's seen any cases yet, hope not. But what if that means it's missed Friendship? You wouldn't trade someone else's happiness for your own, no, but if you *had* to choose?

You don't. And you cling to that on your way down the switchbacked path as if it's some kind of wisdom, though you know it's the opposite.

Back in town, someone's filched a jackknife from the General. Fenton shows you the velveteen gap in the display case, fuming, confused. No one's been in today except for

one of Chase's women, and Harlow Orton to bring a wire,
and he was there no more than a minute and right beside
him the whole time.

"How long's it been missing?" you ask.

Fenton can't remember when he checked last.

"What color was it?"

"Black pearl inlay. Best I carry." He stares at the others as
if they might vanish.

"What did the woman look like?"

"What they all look like. You know."

"Young, old?"

"I don't know," he says. "It was probably one of those
Ramsays, they were in yesterday making trouble."

You'll keep an eye out, you say, though you know you'll
never find it. Fenton's not really upset; it's a risk of the business, spillage. And he's done well for himself, built the store
back up after his father nearly drank it away. He just needs
someone to complain to, and that's you. You linger, make
sure he gets his money's worth, then back at the jail let out
a sigh. These days it seems like you're not getting anything
done.

Doc says the woman probably won't make it till Sunday.
You may have to come in and say something. You say that's
fine. Irma's still in Chicago; Doc's told her to stay put until
this blows over. He peers deep into the green lake of his
blotter as he admits this.

"Blows over," you challenge him.

"It only makes sense."

And it does, that's the thing. It does.

Home is better. Clouds boil up after supper, and you and
Marta walk out back to watch them. You kiss her, smell the
flowery powder on her neck. She's missed you, staying
inside all day. She apologizes for being testy, but it's hard.
She wants to hear everything you've done, as if you've
returned from some lavish expedition. You hold each other
close and look to the sky, hopeful. You need to tell her about
Irma, but you don't. Hold her closer. Clouds pile up and
collide, their dark centers menacing. Leaves flutter, blow
over your withered garden. All month you've been waiting
for rain. If it came down now, you'd dance in it, roll in the
wet grass, sacrifice your clothes. Amelia's asleep and the
evening's yours. Marta kisses you hard, like she used to, and
the wind kicks up.

"Jacob," she says, "come to me now."

"Yes."

"Not here. Inside."

"Here," you say.

"Jacob," she scolds, teasing. "Here?" Then she slips your
jacket off one shoulder and laughs as if it's her idea.

The grass is cool on your arms, the warmth of her stomach shocking, and there's nothing you need, just this, now,
her, always. She challenges you, laughing, then holds you
after, concerned, teary, glad.

It's cooler, the evening deepening. You want to feel the
first drops on your back, this relief a direct consequence of
your love. This drought has to end, things have to get better for Friendship. They're not idle wishes, not desperate
yet. Isn't love a kind of prayer, an act of faith? God's love on

top of yours, or your love a part of God's. Goodness. Hope. Surely—at the very least—there is mercy. Marta kisses your eyelids, and it's true, you really do believe this. You're in love with this world again. The wind rushes over you, roars in the trees, but in the morning the sky's blinding, the leaves calm, and once again you begin the long chain of days.

Friday just before lunch Cyril Lemke comes running in, saying there's a fire out the Shawano road. "Bout a mile past Ender's bridge. I seen the smoke from the bell tower." He stands there panting, winded from his run across town. His hands are white with birdlime, and he's wringing a filthy rag. Cyril's simple, older than Doc but a nine-year-old inside; he licks his lips, blinks like a pigeon.

"Old Meyer's place," you say.

"Far's I could tell." He's shaking, excited by the fire. "What are you gonna do?"

"Spose I'll go see what it is." You want to be calm for him, even if the woods *are* burning. There have been rumors of incendiaries on the loose, of a great fire to the north sweeping through a Winnebago village, leaving nothing but the axles of wagons, the hoops of tubs. Thirty dead, and rumor is the children's throats were cut, their bodies untouched by the fire.

"Need any help?" Cyril asks. "I can pump the water for you." He starts to tell a story to prove he can do it.

"That's all right, Cy, you go ahead. It's almost noon."

It's Cyril's job to ring the hours, to call the town in for

lunch, supper, church. The children tease him, call him
Dumbbell, Ding Dong. Once you saw little Martin Ramsay
walk straight up to him and punch him in the jewels; you
ran over and seized the boy by the throat and later were
ashamed of hurting him. Cyril just held himself, puzzled,
then upchucked.

Now he stands there blankly regarding the clock, the fire
forgotten. You thank him and walk past him to the door,
hoping he'll take the cue, and he does. He watches you away
on your bike, waves the rag athletically.

You don't know what you're going to do if it's the woods.
Get the water engine from the mill, have the hands dig a
line around the fire, keep it out of town. Riding, you don't
remember which way the wind's blowing, or even if it is.
The trees don't say much, which is good.

By Ender's bridge you can smell it, and then you crest
the last hill before Meyer's and there it is—not the woods
but a shed, Old Meyer's smokehouse. The smoke goes
straight up, then above the treetops bends to the south, a
few sparks twisting in the wind. The roof of the shed is
gone, one wall solid flame.

Old Meyer and one of the twins—Thaddeus—are sloshing buckets on it, lugging them from the pump across the
yard. You find another bucket and man the handle, make
sure they always have a full one. The pump creaks, the water
strong and heavy in the piston. The engine your regiment
used to cool the gun barrels felt the same, and there's that
same smell of metal and wet ashes and hot air, the same ache
in your shoulders.

Usually, something like this, you'd just let it burn, but not this summer. And Meyer's angry; he's fighting it like an enemy, swearing blue blazes, his face red as a drunkard's. Thaddeus flits across the grass effortlessly, without a word. Father and son, you marvel, how odd. Lately it seems there are mysteries everywhere, as if you've only just opened your eyes.

It takes a while but the three of you get it done. You stand looking at the destruction while Meyer kicks through the wet wreckage. He's still swearing, Thaddeus beside you, absolutely passive, patient as a dray horse, and you turn to him, in that same instant realizing he's not Thaddeus—he's too calm, too aloof.

"You're Marcus," you say.

"Yes, sir."

"Where's your brother?"

"In bed. He's taken poorly."

"Ain't it the way," Meyer says, kicking a blackened side of meat. "Never around when you need 'im."

"What's wrong with him?"

"Fever a some kind, I don't know. Says his throat hurts him. He won't eat anything, won't take a drink, nothing. Goin' on three days now."

You remember the soldier's cup sliding off the wagon into the grass. In the cellar, before you fit the lid on, you blessed the dead man, nodded solemnly over his gray face. His toes were purple, his insteps green. He could have been a friend, an enemy, a civilian caught in the odd fusillade. The woods were full of them. They bobbed in the swamps.

Women sometimes, children. You learned to love them, to consider them your own flesh, while around you your friends went numb, turned callous and bitter. Times like these you wonder if they were right to take the easy way— as if there's a choice.

"And Bitsi," you ask, because you have to, "how's she?"

"One gets sick, they all do," Meyer says. "You know how that goes. They're young though. They bounce back quick. It's nature's way of toughening them up."

He goes on with his theory, tossing charred boards in a heap, Marcus pitching in. It's like the fire, he says. It's a test to see how much we can put up with. He's philosophical, no longer angry, and you wonder if it's because you're there. He knows you disapprove of rough talk, that you prize thoughtfulness, the search for answers.

One gets sick, they all do. The simplicity of it is stunning, a rock cracking a skull.

"It's like Abraham," he says, citing your last sermon, "or Job." The way he says it, it's almost a question. He looks to you, the preacher, wanting confirmation. And there's nothing you can do but agree with him.

You tell Doc and he gets mad at you.

"You didn't tell Meyer to stay away from them?"

"I told him you'd come take a look at them. Maybe it *is* just a fever."

"You say he's been sick three days." He peers at the scab on his palm as if figuring a sum. "How about the girl?"

You admit you don't know, and he sighs.

"I better get out there then."

You thank him, but he just sits there, he doesn't get up. He lays his hands on the blotter and examines his fingers. "Jacob, while I'm gone, if you could take care of Miss Flynn."

It takes you a second.

Doc helps you out. "I tried to find you but you weren't around."

"Lydia."

"I'd be obliged."

"Of course," you say, then repeat it as the news sinks in. It never fails to move you, to hurt you, no matter how many times you hear it, no matter how little you know the deceased. The deceased. It's a word Mr. Simmons taught you as his apprentice. The soldier in you prefers "the dead"; it's less formal, more physical, and that's the fact of death— it's the body that stops, nothing else.

Doc's still frowning over his hands, and you take advantage of the silence to say a prayer for her, then add one for him, against despair. Like you, he needs to save everyone, takes his losses hard. There's no sense telling him he did his best; he knows that.

"I should go tell Chase," you say.

"He was here. He went to get her something to wear."

"I thought you didn't want me dressing people out."

"I don't," he says. "I tried to explain it to him."

"So what do you want me to do?"

"Just throw the dress in with her. Don't let him see her."

You don't answer because you don't like it. Any of it. The dead deserve respect, the living need to grieve.

"I don't want you bleeding her," Doc orders. "Here, I'll help you with her before I go."

"That's all right," you say. You're used to moving them yourself; it's like wrestling, testing your leverage against their dead weight, but Doc insists, and your knee's still bothering you from Mrs. Goetz. Sometimes, getting up from praying in the empty cell, you hear your tendons creak across your kneecap, then snap back in place.

The room smells of liniment, a blast of vinegar with a touch of horseradish. Doc starts to wrap her in the sheets. Her face is drained, and she seems thinner, the collar of her nightshirt specked with blood, a solid blotch on one shoulder. It seems longer than four days since you've seen her, but it's not. Lydia Flynn, saved from the train stations. Automatically you bow your head to say a few words, and Doc stops and folds his hands.

"Ay-men," he says, then covers her face.

You want to say you can do this, but it's important to him, so you stand back, stay out of his way until he tells you to take her feet. The head's heavier, and by the parlor Doc's face is red. You check the street—nothing but the bright dust, the blank windows of Fenton's General. How many times have you two done this before, and yet it always feels clandestine, as if this were midnight, the two of you murderers, ghouls.

You toe the spittoon aside so the door closes and take her down to the cellar. Turn up the wick of the lamp so you can see what you're doing. On the draining table she seems short, a little over five foot; you've already cut some that length. But not dressing her out seems wrong. It was too hard for you to do the soldier that way. You didn't tell Doc that you bled him, that you rouged his cheeks and combed his hair just so, fit his cap back on before closing the lid. You didn't tell Doc because even he wouldn't understand. Every calling has its demands, its exigencies. In his work, a man makes promises to God.

"I told Chase she'd be here," Doc says from the stairs.

"What about the sheets?"

"Leave them the way they are," he says. "And Jacob, I want you to wear a mask."

You assure him you will, and he leaves, but even after he's closed the door you keep your eye on the knob, sure he's not finished, that he'll come back and tell you everything he's thinking. When he doesn't, you turn to the table and work, then remember the mask. Tying it behind your neck, you wonder what he could have told you that you don't already know, or at least suspect. Still, you want to hear it from him. Why?

You listen to his footsteps cross the floor above your head, then you climb the stairs and lock the door.

Maybe you'd be less afraid if he said it, less alone. But no, this is wrong too. You're not alone, and your fear isn't for yourself but for others. You just want him to say there still may be a chance it'll miss you, when you know there isn't.

You tend to Lydia Flynn. Unwrap the winding sheet, slide the nightshirt over her head. She's tanned on the face and arms, the rest of her lard white. The girl in the station Chase described was stick-thin a waif, but here she seems no different from the town women her age, gone broad with pies and white gravy, the comforts of the hearth. You expect some revelation from her flesh—shackle scars on her ankles, lash marks between her shoulders—but there's nothing untoward save the gray tinge already settling around her mouth. She wears a small cross; it rests in a hollow of her throat.

"Did he save you," you ask, "or did you save yourself?"

Neither, most likely. God doesn't come and sweep you up like a lover, cure you like a doctor. You recognize something, a silence in the middle of noise, a stillness that no matter how fast you run won't go away. Is that it, Lydia?

"What is it like, to go from one world to another like that?"

Strange, frightening. Blissful. Safe. You think of coming home from the war.

"Did it seem real to you at first?"

"I was grateful," you say.

"But no, not real at first. Like a dream. Like a dream I was having."

"And how does it feel now?"

"It's still a dream."

You know you're not supposed to, but you find an empty cask and run a hose to it, make a slit behind her ankle and crank the table so it tilts. You'll be careful; Doc won't know. The blood fills the gutter, drums the bottom of the cask, then after a minute it runs silent, pours like oil. You never talk now; you check the level of the formaldehyde in the white barrel, make sure there's enough. You've never done anyone from the Colony and you want to do a good job for Chase. For Lydia, really. For yourself?

"We are all saved."

"Do you believe that?"

How you want to say yes to this, I do, but there's nothing. You work, and work is praise.

Wait till the blood is just drips, then pump the handle to flush her with water. Now the fluid through its own stained hose, tartly stinking of paraffin thinned with kerosene. Stop the wound with a dollop of hot wax, apologizing as the faint hairs curl and wither around the plug.

You're working on her part, plucking the few gray strands, when someone thumps at the front door. You leave the comb jutting from her hair, on the stairs remember your mask and toss it at your workbench. Before you open the cellar door, you touch your key ring, then set the lock.

It's Chase, with a long white box tied with ribbon. His logger's shoulders fill the window, behind him a team stamping in its traces. You open the door for him and stand aside, but he doesn't come in, just hands you the box with a murmur. He seems tired, defeated, as if, the outcast, he's been proved wrong in front of the whole town and has come for his punishment. Still, he expects you to say something, to comfort him; he's like anyone else, and again you're surprised. Why did you think he'd be different? All these years, you've scoffed at the stories about the Colony—the orgies and devil worship, the midnight sacrifices—knowing how fearful people can be of religion, but maybe some thoughtless part of you believed them, separated Chase and his people from those you love, made them less, expendable.

"I'll make sure everything's just so," you promise him.

"I know you will," he says glumly, and shakes your hand. He asks when he should come around for her.

"Tomorrow morning," you say, though you'll be done by sundown. Doc may have something to say in all this. You'll probably end up accompanying her, making sure the box gets in the ground untouched.

"I'm very sorry," you tell him, and he nods his thanks, lips muttering but saying nothing. He turns to his team and climbs up on the seat.

It doesn't seem enough, and as he starts them off, you want to call after him, tell him how you too question the ways of faith, the injustice, the never-ending losses, that it stuns you too, that you still grieve for Mrs. Goetz and Arnie and Eric Soderholm just as their families do, though everyone else seems to have forgotten. Lydia Flynn, the tramp behind Meyer's, the men in the swamps of Kentucky. If a sparrow fall, you want to say, it is not lost. I will remember. We *are* all saved. But Chase knows this, he must after so many years. It's just a hard moment for him, a low point, not some soul-shaking crisis; you know those aren't sudden or public, they take years, worming inside you like a disease. And anyway, he's gone, lost in his own dust. You close the door and turn away, the box awkward in your arms.

In the basement, you see it's the uniform—the black shift and linen blouse the Colony women wear—and you remember her in the field, how she had on city clothes. You take the comb from her hair, scourging yourself for such disrespect. You remember her stockings and her high-buttoned shoes, just like Irma's.

"Maybe you were running away," you say, and fit her arm through one sleeve. "Maybe you were going to run off with your lover."

"No," you say, "I was coming back in the dark and got lost."

"That late in the day?"

"I was trying to get to the railway station."

"The train doesn't stop here anymore."

"I didn't know that."

"Or the evening stage."

"I didn't know. I just wanted to leave."

"Then where were your bags?"

"They took everything. Even the clothes weren't my own."

"They wouldn't be," you say. "Your old city clothes wouldn't fit."

You pause to contemplate this and see your mask on the floor by the workbench. You knot it on, smell your stale breath trapped in the thin cotton. You turn back to Lydia Flynn and pull the other sleeve up her arm. She's cool beneath your fingers, the last heat of her retreating to a warm core.

"Why city clothes?" you ask, moving, like any penny-dreadful detective, back to your original question.

Is it a mystery? Maybe she was trying to spare the rest of them. Maybe she was out of her head, sick, insane. Afraid.

And why she died isn't a mystery. Still, it's your job to be suspicious. You'd never say it, even to Marta, but you're proud of your ability to both believe and question everything. Secretly you think everyone does, but at some point they give in, surrender to the comfort of certainty. It's too much trouble, this endless jousting of belief and doubt, too tiring. Finally you suppose it will break you, yet strangely it's the only thing that keeps you going—though, true, at times you feel unbalanced, even somewhat mad. Crazy Jacob the Undertaker. A holy fool. Wouldn't your mother laugh at that.

You drape the shift over Lydia, pinch one side under a thigh, then roll her over and fasten it in the back. Tuck the blouse in, fix the collar, her neck still warm against your pinkie. There's no hose, only a homely pair of black socks and a blocky pair of cast-off shoes too big for her, their soles holey, thin as paper.

"There," you say, and retrieve the comb. Her hair's snarled from the sickroom pillow, and then when you work it free, a sprig sticks out. Lick your fingers and wet it, draw the comb across and pat it down. A little pancake for the face. Rouge. Inspect, touch up.

"Very nice."

The coffin won't take long. You don't have to measure anymore, you just naturally head for the right stack of boards. It worries you sometimes; walking down the street or peering out from the pulpit, you size people up, decide who's likely. You worry that you don't have a nice piece of cedar long enough to accommodate Harlow Orton.

Square the corners, drive the nails. The basement's quiet, occasionally a drip from the table. The smell of the lamp and the paraffin when it hits you is dizzying. You pin in the crusted sheets like bunting, fasten them with tacks. Plane the lid so it fits. Muffled, the church bell calls four, then five o'clock, the mill whistle screams quitting time. You think you should get home—you don't want to worry Marta—but you take your time and do it right. Take advantage of it now, you counsel. Make this your best work. You won't have the luxury with Thaddeus and the others.

When you come up it's twilight, the jail wrapped in shadows. The darkness seems hot after the cellar. Your back hurts from lowering her into the box, and you stretch, rolling your neck, pleased to have gotten the job done. You know Chase will be early tomorrow, so you buckle your gun belt, tug your jacket on and head for home.

It's dusk and the bats are circling low above the oaks, the evening star clear as a lantern. You walk through town, the air rich with butter-fried onions, and as you pass your neighbors' warm, orange windows, you see them bent over their plates, discussing the day's events. Marta's promised chicken, and you picture it keeping warm in the oven. It's a superstition of hers, the whole family sitting down to supper. She'll be waiting, distracting Amelia with a song and a piece of zwieback. She'll set everything on the table while you wash up, and when you come back in, she'll be waiting beside Amelia, fixing her bib. You'll sit a moment in silence, the three of you together for the first time since breakfast, the day's business evaporating, becoming, finally, unimportant, and then you'll say grace.

A horse snorts inside the livery, and ahead, under the tunnel of trees, you can see the ghost of another coming up the road. Slowly it reveals itself—Doc's white mare hauling his trap. It rattles and grinds over the stones. You flag him down, but don't go closer. The mare rolls its eyes in the blinders, puffs its rubber lips. They always smell of blood and feces, the rank, wormy meat.

Doc leans over the reins to speak. "Get her ready?"

You say yes but nothing else, and he thanks you. He doesn't ask why you're on the road so late, and you wonder if he knows. Of course he does; he knows you.

"You see Thaddeus?" you ask.

"I saw both of them. You were right. I put a quarantine on the place."

"What about Meyer and the other one?"

"I told them to be careful."

"And the girl?"

Doc looks off up the road as if someone might be coming. He shakes his head, looks at his hands. "There's nothing I can do for them. Just have to wait and see."

Wait and see what? you want to ask, but don't. You've seen what it does. And you know he's doing his best. It reminds you of how sometimes folks will blame you for a crime left unsolved, like Fenton and his jackknife; until you catch someone, it's as if you've robbed them yourself.

"Is he going to put up a sign or do you want me to?"

"I asked him not to," Doc says. "I still want to be careful with this."

"I'd rather be careful the other way. You can say it's chicken pox."

"It's still isolated."

"How many more cases till it isn't?"

"Jacob," he says. "Think. What will people do when they find out?"

"Leave."

"And what if they have it? What if it isn't isolated—and you think it isn't."

You imagine them moving through Shawano and back east toward Milwaukee, splitting off in all directions like spurs from a trunkline.

"I'd rather keep it here," Doc says. "It's easier to just close town off, quarantine the whole thing. That's what they did in St. Joe."

"And it worked," you ask.

"It didn't spread."

"How about inside the town?"

"More than half the town survived."

"Half the town," you repeat.

"*More* than half survived. If it had gotten to Joplin who knows what would've happened."

"What if no one has it except Meyer?"

"Then we're fine," he says.

"What if our other tramp has it and he's in Shawano living it up with some new chums?"

"Then it's Bart's decision, not ours."

The two of you look at each other, trying on arguments. Your head hurts, maybe from the paraffin, maybe from just talking with Doc. All of it, everything. The heat.

"I don't like it," you say.

"Neither do I, but right now we don't have much choice in the matter."

You agree out of habit, then wonder whose decision it is. Legally, you think, it's yours. If you believe he's wrong, why not fight him? Or is it too early? Is he right?

It's not the right time, and you say you'll see him tomorrow.

"Chase'll be in early," you say.

"So will I."

"No rest for the weary."

"No sir," Doc says, and starts the team off. You wave, then turn and walk, and soon you can't hear them.

It's darker under the trees, the stars peeking through the canopy, a hint of hyacinth in the air. Tomorrow's Saturday, and you haven't even begun your sermon. How many ways are there to say have faith? You search your memory for a parable on strength, on trusting the Lord. Abraham and Isaac come to mind, but you just did that last week. Job's overused. Lot. You shake your head and walk on. It'll come, just give it time. Maybe leaf through Matthew after supper, look over your old notes.

Round the bend, and there's your house, the lamp lit, windows warm and orange as your neighbors'. Is it selfish that you give thanks for this, that the sight touches you more deeply—that it seems to mean more—after poor Lydia Flynn? If so, you don't mean to be cruel. And you've done right by her, you made sure of that.

Through the gate and up the walk toward the front door. It'll be good to get this gun belt off, the jacket, the boots. You've earned your supper.

Locked, just as you instructed. You jangle the big key ring, searching.

Open the door and the light blinds you. Fresh bread, and the salty crackle of fat. On the floor of the sitting room lies Amelia's stuffed duck, toppled on its side. You undo the gun belt—Marta won't have it around the child—and stow it high in the front closet, thumping the door shut to announce yourself. When no one comes, you make your way to the kitchen.

It's empty, a wisp of steam floating up through a hole in the stove top.

"Marta," you call.

In the dining room the table's set, your milk poured, the high chair between the two seats so you can each minister to her. The tray holds a spray of crumbs, a slug of gravy. Maybe they couldn't wait.

The back of the house is dark.

"Marta?"

You try your room first, peering in the door. She's not on the bed, and immediately you turn to the nursery.

It's black, and you have to leave the hallway before you see Marta sitting in the rocking chair, her hair a bright frame, her face dark, impossible to read. She's still, hands in

her lap. Amelia's in her crib, already asleep, and softly you
go to Marta.

"I'm sorry," you apologize, ready to explain why, but she
doesn't take your hands, she doesn't look at you, as if you've
done something inexcusable. A wet sniff and you know she's
been crying.

"What is it?"

"She's sick," she says.

"What do you mean?" you ask, though you already know.
Better than anyone, you know.

"She's sick," Marta says, and now she's clutching at you,
grabbing, crushing herself to you with a strength you find
frightening. "Jacob, she's *sick.*"

4

In the dark you hear Amelia coughing, then Marta's soft footfalls. You slip out of bed and stand in the door in your nightshirt, watching her bend over the crib. She rearranges the blankets, returns to the rocker and waits.

"Come to bed," you whisper.

"No."

"I'll see to her."

"No, you go on."

It's been like this all night. You've already warned her that it's dangerous, that she needs her rest. You argue, then retreat. You wouldn't think of keeping her from Amelia. Maybe it's just a summer cold. You'll get Doc to take a look at her in the morning.

Till then, you lie awake in the half-empty bed, each cough startling you like a gunshot. You think of your sermon, of what you can possibly say now that would be true. You do believe Amelia will get better. And if she doesn't, what will that do to your faith? Is it so weak that the sorrows of this world can destroy it with one puff? You hope not, but maybe so. Maybe so.

You think of the night you first saw Marta—at a barn dance in Shawano—how, like now, you couldn't sleep afterward, how it seemed that her grin and the cock of her slim hips threw your whole world in doubt. She danced herself into a sweat, and when you tried to take her by the waist—primly, oh, with the most noble intentions—she kicked you in the shin and whirled away laughing. Though you'd spoken only a few words to her, you felt—you hoped and feared both—that soon you'd be leaving behind everything you knew. It was exciting, and frightening, and while that's not quite how it feels tonight, you recognize this new edge the two of you have stepped over.

But that was willful, you think. This is different.

Faith will always save you. In the dark you repeat the phrase to yourself, as if that will make you believe it. It's a question, really, and you think the answer could make a good sermon. When won't faith save you?

When you believe too much in this world. In yourself. In anything but God.

When you won't let it. When you don't want to be saved.

And why wouldn't you want to be saved?

Because you don't deserve to be.

Those nights during the siege, it was this quiet. You'd lost track of the days, cut your thumb peeling strips of meat from the horse's jaw. You had to feed the little Norwegian; he couldn't walk from hunger. His teeth fell out in clumps, his hair took a reddish tint. At night you stood guard with an empty rifle, bayonet fixed, listening to the wet suckling of lips. In the morning, the dying accused you of having food.

A cough, and Marta crosses the room. Amelia wheezes. You wait till it ends, then get up, your nightshirt fighting you, binding you tight as you toss the heavy feather tick aside.

Marta has the lamp lit, the wick so low the flame paints her chin blue above the crib. She lays the back of her hand against Amelia's head, then tucks the coverlet up to her neck and turns to you, a hand on the rail.

"How is she?" you ask.

"Hot. She's due for a feeding but I don't want to wake her."

"She'll be fine," you say, and Marta nods. She understands you have to say this, that you have to believe.

"Go back to sleep," she says. She pads to the rocker and sits down, tips her head back and closes her eyes. "Go."

You want to do it just to agree with her, to make things easier. There's nothing to say, no appropriate biblical wisdom, though you could quote Scripture till the sun comes up. And so you go to your knees beside the crib.

You don't have to ask Marta to join you, merely close your eyes and bow your head, and soon you hear her cross the rug and kneel beside you. Her hand takes yours, cool, and the two of you concentrate, beseeching Him, pledging your honest faith though you know it's nothing in His eyes and that you'll accept His will regardless because you're His servants.

Amelia barks, stopping you. Her throat rattles, full of stones. The two of you wait till it's just scraps, then whistling breath. You go on.

You know He is just and merciful and that there is a purpose in all His works, even this. You ask this in the name of His Son, Jesus Christ, who was crucified for your sins, and in that equation, that sacrifice—Christ's willing death for your sins—you see the hope of all this balancing out, of some justice or salvation from what seems pain and chaos. You believe.

"Amen," Marta says, and squeezes your hand, then sends you to bed. This time you go.

And yet, do you sleep?

Marta's rocker squeaks, and far off, a dog shouts out an alarm. The woods are full of tramps moving through. You think of Old Meyer tending Bitsi and Thaddeus, Lydia Flynn in your cellar. You consider the possibility that you've given it to Amelia, that as you loved Marta in the grass last night, you were killing her. Amelia hasn't been out of the house in days. You dragged the dead man by his ankles, had Thaddeus lift him by the armpits. You set Clytie afire, breathed the meaty smoke. Now Amelia's sick. What other explanation is there?

You get up and go into the other room. Marta looks up, startled, as if she's been sleeping.

"It must be me," you say. "I've given it to both of you."

"Go back to bed," she says.

"I'm sure of it."

"Jacob."

"No," you say, and confess everything, kneeling at her feet. She leans over and holds you, her hair falling across your face, catching in your tears. Your pride, your carelessness, your sentimental love for the dead. It's all true.

"But you're fine," she reasons, "I'm fine. It might be a cold after all. We won't know until Doc looks at her."

"And if it is?"

"If it is," she starts, but doesn't finish.

You look up at her, find her eyes. She's always been stronger than you. Why is this a surprise?

"If it is," she says, "then it is."

Though you hold each other, it isn't comforting, and when you're back in bed, alone, the moon seems bright on the wall above the commode, the shadow of the empty basin a dark blossom, the lamp a twisted stalk. The portrait of Amelia that Irma painted for her birthday is obscured, faceless, a framed blot. Marta coughs now, heavier than Amelia, and measured. You get up and move to your desk, lean over a blank sheet of paper in the gray light. Uncap the ink, dip the nib. Again, what can you say that is absolutely true?

It is not ours to question God's will.

There is a reason for our suffering.

You dismiss these immediately, don't even write them down. We will always question God's will. We will always need a reason for our suffering.

Something about mercy.

Amelia coughs and Marta moves to the crib.

Mercy, you write, then hesitate.

Is that all we can ask for? And even then there's no guarantee. What does faith entitle us to?

Nothing. And in that lies its purity.

Can you really say this? You picture your congregation lifting their faces, chins tipped up, waiting for you to start. Doc, John Cole and his family, Yancey Thigpen, Millie Sullivan. And what can you say to Old Meyer? Marta? Chase?

"Jacob," Marta whispers from the door. "You're talking to yourself again."

You nod, apologetic, and she leaves you. Usually she'd joke with you, ask if you're wrestling with angels, but not tonight—or this morning, as your pocket watch reminds you, its ticking amplified by the desktop. In two hours the sun comes up.

Mercy.

You nudge the sheet of paper away, cap the ink and blot the quill. Stand and let out a cough.

It's just a rumble, a speck catching in the skin of phlegm coating your throat, the air tearing its way back up and out of your mouth. Briefly, gone before you can raise a fist to stanch it. That's it, just the one. You lift the feather tick and slide in, then lie there in the moonlight, wondering if all three of you are sick, until, perversely, you're sure it would be best for everyone. Board yourselves in and die together. You'd be the last, that way you could take care of them. Oddly, the thought eases you.

And still you don't sleep. You won't, you know, and so you lie there trying to come up with a first line for your sermon. It's obvious what you're going to talk about; avoiding it would be pointless, coy. The question is, what can you possibly say to help them?

You're still trying out first lines when you hear Fred Lembeck's rooster. He calls and calls. You're not going to sleep anyway. A spider's working in the corner of the window. The sun's not up yet, the sky deepening to blue in the east, the morning star low over the horizon. It's cool enough for dew, and the tracks of something have dragged a dark path across the yard. Beyond the garden, the trees are noisy with birds.

Marta comes in from the other room, bleary and yawning, taking baby steps. "She's still asleep," she reports, and lies down.

"I'll be quiet."

"When does Doc open?" She keeps her eyes closed.

You explain about Chase coming in for the woman.

She opens her eyes and gets up, starts going through her wardrobe. You follow her lead.

"I can take her if you want to rest," you say, but just for form's sake.

Marta ignores you, chooses a blue blouse you love. You button up beside her, the two of you silent, concentrating on getting dressed. Your belt buckle jingles and clinks; her petticoats rustle. You catch her eye as if you have something to say, and she stops brushing her hair, waits, her hand cocked. But what is there to say? She tips her head again and pulls the brush through, tearing out hair with a ripping sound. She pinches a wad from the bristles and drops it above the trash basket, and the dead cloud floats down.

"I'm sure it's just a cold," you say, and immediately the heat of shame—of trespassing—flares through you.

"Let's hope," she says, but bitterly, and you promise not to do this to her again.

You put on coffee, your one concession to the usual routine. Neither of you can stomach it. Any other day you'd pour it back in the pot, but now you wait till she goes to wake Amelia, then open the window and dump both cups out on the ground.

"What was that?" Marta asks when she returns.

Rather than answer her, you take Amelia in your arms and hold her to you. She surfaces a minute, still dreaming. Those too-blue eyes, all Marta. She's warm, and her breath flutters wetly in your ear. Her lungs seem to squeak. It's just a cold. Doc will know.

She coughs and fusses, grumps, nearly waking up.

"It's all right, honey," you murmur, and sway to quiet her. "Papa's right here. Yes, that's better, you hush now, yes."

Marta's about to take her back so you can get your jacket on when you hear the bells. Seven o'clock. Doc should be in by now. You hand Amelia over and go to the front hall closet. You palm the doorknob, and the church bell rings.

You turn as if you can see the bell tower from here. Cyril rings it again, lets it reverberate away into birdsong. Marta looks to you, confused, though you both know it means a woman has died. Her eyes ask if you know anything; you just shrug, puzzled.

Neither of you move as it tolls out the age of the dead. You count. Twenty-six. Twenty-seven. Amelia clenches a tiny fist, then lets it fall, drops back into sleep. Fifty-one, fifty-two. It goes on, preposterously, and you wonder if Cyril has lost track (but no, that's not Cyril; he's precise to a fault, his child's mind exacting, inflexible).

Then suddenly it stops.

"Seventy-six," Marta checks, and you nod yes.

"Elsa Sullivan."

"Poor thing."

You don't want to appear cruel, but you need to get Amelia in to see Doc, and you turn and open the door. You can talk about Elsa on the way. Doc probably has her laid out in back by now.

It's brilliant out—as it has been all month. You step aside to let Marta by, and the bell tolls again.

You both stop on the walk.

Twice, another woman.

Cyril chimes out her life. The two of you stand there; it would be disrespectful to move. You count to seventy-three.

"Millie," Marta guesses.

You know she's right, but it doesn't make sense. Elsa you've already conceded. Millie's still strong.

Marta crosses herself and then Amelia's forehead. Usually you'd ask each other what could have happened—a fire maybe—but not today. Before the last knell has faded away, you've opened the gate and started off for town. And then the bells stop you again.

One.

"Jacob," Marta beseeches you in the long pause, and you put an arm around her, squeeze her shoulder, the two of you standing there, facing the distant steeple, counting.

Thirty-eight.

There are a few possibilities—Fenton, Carl Huebner, Gillett Condon—but neither of you say their names. You walk fast, as if Cyril might stop you again. You wonder why Doc didn't come and get you. The dust is thick and hard to walk in. A Menominee family creaks by in a wagon heaped with provisions, blankets, furniture, a skinny cow trailing behind. A minute later, a second family with the same cow, the father laughing deeply at something, making the best of the move. It reminds you of the retreat after the siege, everyone desperately grateful, a little wild.

Outside the livery, in a ditch, one of Austin Phillips's dogs lies on its side, flies swarming its eyes, the peach pit of its behind. Marta flinches, covers her mouth with a hand, turns as if to shield Amelia from the stink. If it's not gone by lunch, you'll have to ask Austin to bury it, under penalty of fine, and you don't want to do that.

Finally you reach the sidewalk. You expect to see Chase's rig under Doc's shingle, and people, a confusion of loved ones, but there's only Doc's trap.

Inside, Fred Lembeck sits on the love seat, hunched over his barn boots, his one hand on his knees, as if leaning into a campfire. He lost the other arm to the leather belt of a thresher, but it hasn't slowed him down any. He's not like Bart, though; you've never heard him joke about it. He stands when he sees Marta, nods. He frowns solemnly as he greets you.

"It's the girls," he confirms, and you say you're sorry. While Fred and them weren't close, they were neighbors, and that's something.

"Who else?"

"Morning, Jacob," Doc calls from in back. "I figured you'd hear Cyril."

You holler back, and Amelia wakes up and complains. You ask Fred again.

"Austin Phillips," he whispers, as if to protect Marta.

"Austin Phillips?" both of you echo, and instinctively you turn to her as if she might have an answer. She doesn't.

"We saw one of his dogs on the road," you say, but the clue goes nowhere. The three of you stand there, dumb. Austin Phillips has been the town farrier since before the war. His father was the town smith, and his father before him, an old Indian fighter.

Doc comes through the curtain, drying his hands on a towel. He sees Marta and pauses, a hitch in his step on his way to the desk. He half-bows, dips his head in acknowledgment, then checks your faces, looks at Fred.

"Austin Phillips," you question him.

Doc nods. "Last night. Fred here found Millie and Elsa this morning."

"Before chores," Fred says, and again all of you stare speechlessly at Irma's beautiful Persian carpet.

"I just saw Millie the other day," you say.

"I know," Fred says, just as baffled.

Doc turns to Marta to change the subject. "You brought Amelia."

"She's sick." Marta moves to the desk, holding Amelia out like an offering, and you're forgotten. Fred sits down again, leans his one elbow on his knee.

"What seems to be the problem?" Doc asks, and Marta tells him everything.

He moves his paperweight aside and lays Amelia on the blotter, turns up the lamp to look at her throat. Amelia wails. He ignores it, his face hovering above hers, his mouth grim as he concentrates. He sees something, you can tell by the way he squints and pinches his lips together, the way he goes still as a hunter.

And then suddenly he straightens up, done with that. He peeks up her nose, slips a pinkie between her gums. She shrieks, her whole head red, a faint tracery of veins under the thin skin. Marta looks to you, unsure, and Doc shifts Amelia on the blotter, pulls the lamp closer. He leans across her, and you find yourself moving to get a better view. Her tiny eyebrows are white, her hands opening and closing on nothing.

He has her jaws propped open, shifting his head from side to side, pinning her tongue down with his thumb. Amelia gags and hacks. He goes still again, holds his breath a second.

"All right, you," he says softly, lifting Amelia off the

blotter, not quite satisfied, and bites his bottom lip in thought. Amelia's screaming. Doc holds her in the crook of his shoulder and pats her back, but it doesn't work, and he returns her to Marta.

Amelia quiets, whimpering, then coughs and settles, Marta cuddling her, soothing her with words.

Doc slides the paperweight to the center again, but doesn't let go, as if contemplating the move. Chews his bottom lip. He still won't look at you.

"Why don't we come on in back and get a better look," he says.

How can he possibly get a better look, you wonder, and though you want to know right now—does she have it, yes or no—though you want to protest, both of you silently agree and start to follow him through the curtain.

He stops and you nearly run into him. "Marta, if you could wait out here with her, just a minute."

"All right," she says, but she looks to you frantically, as if she doesn't understand why she's being left behind. You try to calm her with a nod, then do it too quickly.

"Jacob," Doc says, and you follow him in.

He closes the door to the first room before you can see who's in it. The hall is filled with that fatty, familiar smell, and you think of Lydia Flynn in her box, Chase on the way. Goddamn this thing.

Elsa's in the second room, on the bed, wrapped in a sheet, a patch of striped nightgown peeking out.

Before you reach the third door, Doc turns to you. He

lays a hand on your shoulder and pulls you close as a lover, leans his lips to your ear. You can smell the minty brilliantine in his hair.

"She swallowed half a bottle of Paris green. You know what that does to someone?"

"It burns." Bart had a man once, a millwright, drank a glass of the insecticide to toast his bankruptcy. Bart still talks about it, almost joking, worst thing he's ever seen.

"You ever see it?"

"No," you confess.

"I want to cover her if that's all right."

He leaves you in the dim hall. At the far end the same spray of sun plays on the wallpaper. You remember seeing it only a few days ago, commenting on it, but what you were feeling then seems distant, almost lost. Compared to Amelia, it seems frivolous, and for an instant you hate it, and yourself for noticing.

"All set," Doc says, beckoning you.

He's laid a clean towel over her face. She's wearing the same heavy dress, the same boots the Ramsay boys used to make fun of. First Clytie, now her. You think of their place empty, the withered garden, the listing porch. You liked the quiet there, the back door open on the yard. You say a prayer and take her ankles, careful not to touch the skin.

"Looks like she gave half to Elsa," Doc says, maneuvering her through the door. "Fred found her in the kitchen. Elsa was up in bed. He's a little shook up."

"Naturally."

You're quiet in the hall. Doc walks backward, then turns

at the second door. You can feel her feet through the boots. Probably already swelling. You'll have to cut the laces away, peel the leather like rind. If he lets you, that is. Probably not.

There's not enough room on the bed for both of them, so you bend over and lay her on the floor. As you do, the towel falls off her face, and for the first time you see what Paris green does to someone.

Her lips are gone, carved away, along with most of her throat. The skin around it isn't burnt but neatly sliced, livid, the layers of fat and gristle plain as a Sunday roast. You can see where the roots of her teeth meet the jaw, and all you can think of is the siege—the sun coming up on the dead, the strips of flesh gouged out and nibbled in the dark.

You use the Lord's name.

Doc whisks the towel over her. "You all right?"

"God have mercy."

"There're easier ways," Doc agrees.

He lifts you under one arm, moves you to the door, then shuts it firmly. Amelia, you think, you need to worry about her—but Millie's teeth. Her feeding it to Elsa like medicine. You pray she didn't stay to watch. You imagine what it must have done to their stomachs.

There's no time. Doc parts the curtain and ushers Marta in. She stalks by the two of you, impatient with waiting, being left out of the secret. You trail her past the two closed doors, glimpse the green sunlight still shimmering on the wall.

Across from the bed there's a commode as high as a sideboard, and Doc has Marta lay Amelia on its wide top. She paws the air, trying to find her mother. He lights a lamp, gives it some wick, then a second one. Marta takes your hand. He strips Amelia's shift off and presses two fingers to her chest, her neck, searches for her glands. You scan his face for the littlest hint; he seems satisfied but still grim, purposefully reserved. From a drawer he takes a cotton swab and a kind of jeweler's loupe and leans over her, only her kicking feet visible. He leans in and fishes around her mouth with the swab, dips his shoulder to use the light. Amelia chokes and cries and Marta squeezes your hand; you squeeze back to reassure her—or are you pooling your terror, adding it to hers?

Doc pulls back and motions the two of you over, keeping a hand on Amelia's chest. He holds the swab up to one lamp. It's tipped with blood.

Neither of you have to ask. There's the proof, irrefutable. And though you know what it means, you can't understand it. You stand there like a man confronting a loaded gun for the first time. There must be something you can do. Leave. Flee.

"I'm afraid it is," he says.

"Yes" is your first word, just as Marta's is "No."

She looks to you as if you can change this. You have to. It's your fault, you know it is, it's all your fault.

"She has what's called a thrush on the back of her throat," he explains, feeling his own. "You can see how sensitive it is; I barely touched it with this."

"It can't be a cold," you ask. "Or a sore throat."

He shakes his head gently.

"She's just a baby," Marta says.

Doc apologizes, trying to comfort you. He gathers Amelia and presents her to Marta, snuffs the lamps with two quick twists, slips the loupe into the drawer.

"What can we do?" you ask.

Doc pauses—stiff, gentlemanly. It seems he's stalling, hoping you'll pitch in, rescue him. You've seen him do this before, when he doesn't have an answer. When there is no answer.

"Try to keep her comfortable," he says.

"What does that mean?" Marta says. "Isn't there medicine? Isn't there something she can take?"

"I'm sorry," he says again.

Marta sways with Amelia, her lips grazing her sparse hair. You hold her the same way, take strength from the smell of her. She shakes her head, still not believing him. But there's the swab, the bright, wet tip.

It won't be long, Doc says. In children it progresses quickly. It's already rather advanced, he's afraid.

You appreciate the way he says this—apologetic, respectful. He knows these words aren't enough. He would rather be telling you anything else. You know how it feels; you've done this too.

Marta sags in your arms. "Jacob."

"We'll take care of her," you say, when you want to say everything will be all right. It won't be, you know that now, you have to admit it. It's not a lack of faith; you've seen Millie, and Lydia Flynn. All Marta has is Doc's word.

"Jacob," she pleads.

And what are you supposed to do? You want to go home. You want to give up. You want to rage against God for what He's done. You want to beg Him.

There's nothing to do. You've been in the business long enough to understand grief. That's the awful thing: there is nothing to do but go on. You don't want to, you don't want to leave the loved one behind, but you do. Death's taught you that much at least.

You hold on to Marta.

"I can give you some valerian to help her sleep," Doc offers, and Marta quickly accepts. It's almost a relief, just having some business to attend to.

Up front, a bell jingles, someone coming in from the street, the glass door rattling.

Doc rummages through a cupboard of clinking bottles like an apothecary, finally handing you a vial full of a clear tincture. No, please, he says, you don't need to pay him. He gives you masks to wear when you're tending her.

On the way out, he closes the door. As you walk down the dim hall, he lays a hand on the back of your neck, and it chills you. Suddenly you understand everything you couldn't in the room. It really is going to happen.

Marta ducks through the curtain, Amelia looking back at you from her shoulder. She smiles, toothless, and you try to make a funny face. It's mad, you think. She seems fine.

Expecting Chase, you're surprised to find that Sarah Ramsay and her four boys have taken over the love seat, little Martin on the floor, his hair a rat's nest. Fred Lembeck's gone, Gavin Ramsay laughing and menacing his brothers with one limp sleeve, his arm tucked inside his shirt. Tyrone coughs, and his mother clamps a handkerchief over his mouth. She sees Amelia.

"Whatever it is, they've all got it," Sarah tells Doc, almost joking at her motherly bad luck. She's gone through two husbands, both drinkers, and lives off the insurance money. You want to say you're sorry, but Marta turns from them and hurries for the door. Outside, Chase is just pulling up.

"Here he is," you warn Doc.

"That's all right. He'll just have to wait."

"I can take care of him," you say, though he knows you're not really offering.

"You go home," he orders, and you do.

It's hotter outside, and blinding. Chase is dressed in an elegant mourning coat and a matching top hat, both trimmed with dust. You explain that the baby's sick, and he agrees completely, wards off your apology.

The dog's still there, flies sipping its eyes.

Marta hurries along with Amelia cradled in both arms, slips into the shade of the oaks. You rush to catch up and drape a hand about her waist, and you see she's crying.

"You were going to stay there," she accuses you. "You were going to leave me alone with her."

"I was trying to be polite, that was all."

Amelia coughs, part of the argument.

"That awful Ramsay woman. Four of them."

Again you hold her, but what can you say? Amelia's death seems a shared failure, yet the two of you are separated by it, stand on opposite sides of the chasm, unable to say anything comforting.

"I love you," you say.

"Yes," she says, but dismissively, as if it's inconsequential or off the point; it's not what you're talking about. She turns from you, and you let her go. You follow.

Home, you distract Amelia with zwieback while Marta gives her the drops in a bottle of clabbered milk, then get her settled. The medicine works. The two of you watch her sleep, the birdlike rise and fall of her tiny chest, her lips wet at the edges. Blue veins twine around the pipe of her throat. Thrush. A bird. The Winnebago say the owl is a messenger of death. Doc said it would be quick, and yet it seems so far off. She could be sick, nothing more. Not even that, just sleeping. Marta's hands rest on the rail; she lets you cover them with yours.

"You can go help him if you want," she concedes.

"No," you say, then thank her. She knows you feel bad for leaving Doc with all the responsibility; you know that soon enough you'll have to go back to work. Soon enough. What does that mean—when Amelia's dead? It frightens you how practical you can be, how cold, even with your own. Maybe the schoolhouse rumors are true: maybe you *are* crazy.

You pull a kitchen chair into the nursery, and the sun inches across the carpet. Marta reads while you try to write the sermon you've been avoiding. Your congregation waits. How many now, without Austin? You know the rows, you can see their faces lifted to you. How many are already sick?

You should have called for a quarantine; you shouldn't have listened to Doc.

"You should wear your mask," you tell Marta, but don't press when she says no.

The two of you sit there listening for a hitch in Amelia's breathing. Outside, the oaks sigh, a lone rig passes— probably Chase with Doc along, or Sarah Ramsay carting her boys home. Otherwise, the silence is like night. Though it's market day, Friendship's quiet. It's the end of threshing, you think, and picture the brilliant fields, the glint of reaping scythes. You wish you were riding your bike out along the dusty roads, even in this heat.

Turn to the empty sheet in front of you. The Ramsays sit in the back row. What can you possibly say to comfort them?

You had the same question when you first started apprenticing with Mr. Simmons. You knew about working with the bodies, you were used to that, but what did you say to the families? Tell them the truth, he said. Tell them you're sorry and that you've done your best.

You hope no one comes.

No, that's not true.

Marta shushes you.

Amelia stirs, whimpering, and Marta picks her out of the crib and sits with her, rocks her in her arms. She kisses her forehead and you think of the masks.

"She's warm," Marta says, and you go over to feel her.

Her hair's damp.

You mention the mask again

"You're not wearing yours," she argues, and it's true. Neither of you have to ask why.

You sit again, lick the nib. Marta rocks. She doesn't seem to be reading; the page never turns. The house is cool with the blinds pulled, the rooms gray. The doors are locked, and the rest of Friendship's far away, baking in the heat. Only the three of you here in your little world. To be with them is enough, and you think of Millie Sullivan trudging up the stairs with her bottle of Paris green, and for an instant—even with the vision of her ruined face insisting you reject her solution—you understand what she did.

You look to Marta, rocking, Amelia asleep in her arms. You wonder how long it took for Elsa to get half the bottle down. After the siege, you piled the bodies on ammunition carts, one layer facing one way, the next across it, like sheaves of wheat. Your mother died of a heart attack while reading. When they finally broke into the house, her hands were folded over her Bible, one finger keeping her place.

That's it. Yes, especially now.

"Shhh," Marta says, and you nod, sorry, and pinch your lips together.

You bend to the page and write: *What is the best way to die?*

5

Softly, in the dark. Along the far edge of the churchyard, the valise bulky under one arm. The steeple reaches its finger into the night sky. Cyril's long gone home, the telegraph closed, Fenton's shuttered up. Still, you keep to the weedy traces, navigate the shadowy alley behind Ritter's boarding-house, then slip between the livery and the jail in the steamy reek of horse piss. Take a peek at Main Street, the key sweaty in your hand.

No one, only dust. A dark lump—Austin Phillips's dog. It's your job now, all the things no one wants to do. You have to, it's part of the bargain.

Climb onto the sidewalk and your boots clonk. You fumble with the lock, then push through. Inside, everything sounds loud. Set the valise on your desk and change keys, go open the cellar. You kneel and shield a candle, picture Marta in her rocker, finally quiet, exhausted with sobbing. She didn't argue with you, told you to go, to come back as fast as you can. She hasn't slept since Saturday, and when you asked her, you could see she didn't understand. But she believes in you, she knows you'll do what's best for everyone.

Downstairs you notice you don't have enough cedar, or nothing cut the right size. You can crop the two long ones; it's a waste, but you can't use white pine for this. Fashion a lid out of the scrap, a solid bottom.

"It'll do," you say.

The draining table's flat, a mask limp on your workbench. Light another candle, and your blades flash on the wall, your saws. You take your best rip down and inspect the cedar, run your thumb over the whorled grain. Measure the length against your forearm, then check it again. How often do you have to remind yourself to make this your finest work?

It's seasoned wood, but it cuts tough as red gum, worries your arm like green sycamore. You're tired; Marta's not the only one who hasn't slept. Yesterday, sleepless, you held services for the few who did come. Most from outside town. Cyril. You felt as if you'd tricked them, that you should have given them some sort of warning. Instead you delivered your sermon as written, then met them at the door, exhorting them to be careful.

"It's not the sickness that frets me," Emil Bjornson said, "it's that fire up above us."

Dull, at first you thought he meant the sun, then understood. You wanted to ask him if he had news of the fire, but just said the Lord would sustain us. He agreed because you're the preacher, not from any real belief.

Is it true? In all this—*after* all this—will the Lord sustain us?

"It's not your place to ask that," you say, and the blade neatly cleaves the cedar in two.

Another, then the end pieces. The cellar's cool, and the sweat sits on your neck like a clammy hand. You promise when you get done with this you'll pour yourself a horn of whiskey.

"Just a small one."

Fish in the drawer for eight straight nails. Start cutting the bottom.

You're doing things backwards, you think, but it doesn't stop you. Just get it done. You don't want to leave Marta alone too long.

You want to carve the top. Her name, and the dates. Maybe if there's time later. But you know there won't be.

There's a spot in the garden the crab apple leans over.

What else do you need? You cast around the room, scourging yourself for being so thick-witted. It's like a nervous sickness; your thoughts don't stop long on anything, flit off like a nest of swallows.

Tubing. A cask of fluid. Catgut.

You snap the valise open.

It feels wrong to you, doing it this way. At first you wanted to argue with her, thought she'd lost her mind. No, just grief-stricken; you understand her perfectly. Because that was how you felt. Still feel. And then you saw how it would be easier if the rest of Friendship didn't know, and you softened, let her go on holding her, rocking, whispering in her ear.

The top and bottom are the hardest to get in. The pieces fit, the cask. You wrap the catgut around the nails so they don't clink, fold the tubing over and snap the bag shut. Go around and blow the candles out, all but one.

Will there be anything harder than this? No, and that's almost a comfort. Almost, though honestly you can't imagine anything ever being a comfort again.

She's in Heaven, yes. You do still believe. But it's different now, isn't it?

Friendship's empty, Austin's dog untouched. You drop into the shadows of the alley, the valise heavy under one arm, then cross the back of the churchyard. In His hand, they sleep, all those you've served, blessed, tended. You want to believe this is no different, that you've loved them like a Christian, all equally.

But practically, your actions prove you wrong. You never took any of them home with you. How do you think this is going to help? What good will it do? And who, a better constable might ask, is this man stealing through the night with a mortician's kit under his arm? And why is he crying?

Marta refuses to give her to you.

"No," she says, and won't explain.

She doesn't have to. You go pour that horn of whiskey, drink it standing in the kitchen. You wonder how Meyer is right now, and the Ramsays. Folks all around town, Doc says. This morning he put off calling a quarantine for another day, and again you felt it was your job, that as constable you should overrule him. Tomorrow, for certain. You'll wire down the line and let Bart know. There's no sense risking Shawano when it can be kept in Friendship.

You wonder if it took Amelia for you to make this decision, if it should have been done well before this point.

"Maybe so."

You set your glass on the melodeon and reach into the valise, maneuver the top and bottom through, then the rest. You don't want Marta to hear, so you go out back by the henhouse, where there's no light. With every blow, the chickens stir. Under the moon you fit the top on, the raw cedar white as bone. You have time to carve her name, but you've left your chisels in the cellar.

"Hold on," you say, and fish for your knife.

It's heavy, but everything is tonight. Only when you unfold the long blade do you notice that it's not yours. Maybe a boy's you confiscated and forgot. But no. It winks, and even in the silvered dimness you can see the perfect virgin edge, the liquid shimmer of the black pearl inlay.

It sits in your hand like evidence, yet you hardly remark on it. "Curious" is all you say.

What are the possibilities? That someone else slipped it in your pocket after church. Immediately you think of Cyril, his shack crammed with discarded pots and flaking newspapers. No, he's too slow. But none of the others come from town. You don't remember leaving your jacket anywhere, but you must have. Doc's maybe. You've been so distracted lately that anything's possible.

You angle the top across your lap so it catches the moon and slowly score her name into the new wood. Patience makes good work, Mr. Simmons used to say, and you still listen to him. When it was time to tend him, you made sure his fingernails were trimmed, that he had his Mason's ring. Would he be proud of you now, sticking them in the ground helter-skelter?

"Your own blood."

Calm down. Stop breathing so hard. Start on the letters again.

What are you going to say to Marta?

Here. We should let her rest. It's only proper.

You should be with her now, you think, but go on carving, finish the lid as the moon rises and hangs and starts to fall, and the chickens sleep.

Dew on the yard. The nursery window's still lit, and when you step inside, the house smells of the lamp. Your half-full glass on the melodeon surprises you.

Marta's in the rocker, Amelia in her arms, her face unchanged, only a spot of blood on her jumper. Both of them could be asleep.

Marta coughs, and Amelia's head falls off her arm, lolls back heavy on her neck. You kneel and fit her against Marta, then stay there, unable to wake her. You rest your head on her knee and close your eyes.

"Is it ready then?" she asks clearly, without a trace of sadness.

You answer her softly, wanting her—perversely—to go back to sleep. Who wants to let go? No one. You want the three of you to be together now, but she rocks forward to stand up, and you have to move.

"Where is it?"

"In the kitchen. I'll need her a minute. You could get her something to wear."

"Her christening gown."

"That would be good."

"And her necklace from Aunt Bette." She turns to your room as if to go get it.

"I'll take her," you say, arms wide, and she stops and has a long last look, kisses Amelia on the lips.

She hands her to you, and you're surprised how warm she feels. Marta still doesn't want to leave her, but you tell her to go, that you'll only be a little while, and she does, almost gratefully.

In the kitchen, when you lay Amelia on the table and kiss her forehead, you find that only one side of her is warm.

Her fingers are curled. You slip her arms out of her sleeves, undo her dry diaper. Her skin is bright in the lamplight, perfect except her raw nostrils, the lump of a gland. You reach in the valise and the instruments clink.

You've forgotten a funnel, and have to use Marta's. It doesn't take long, covers just the bottom of the tub. Quick and pitch it in the bushes around the house, rinse it at the creaking pump. Mr. Simmons said some men ask half price for children but that it's customary to do them for free. Christian and good business too. Their small bodies. You think of Arnie Soderholm, Bitsi Meyer. It takes the little ones first, Lydia Flynn said. Why didn't you listen to her?

No wax either, so you open Fenton's knife and slice off the butt of a candle, hold it over her ankle till it seals the wound. A single catgut stitch in each eyelid to hold them open, then gently return everything to the valise. You hide it in the closet before calling Marta.

Yes, you're sure it's good work.

"Thank you, Jacob" is all she says. Bitterly. Resigned. Why can't you say anything to her?

She bends over Amelia and fits her christening gown on, struggling with the cuffs. She can't fasten the clasp of the necklace, and it falls to the floor.

"Help me," she says, and you do. Her fingers shake as you take it from her, and you see she's been gnawing at them.

Fix the clasp and turn it so it's hidden. Except for one eye drifting in, she could almost be alive. You don't say this.

"She looks very pretty," Marta says, but uncertainly, and again you wish you knew what she's really thinking. "Can she lay out in the parlor, or is it too warm? With the sickness I suppose it's not a good idea."

"No," you reluctantly agree.

"Then let's do it now while I'm feeling able."

You go to her and hold her. So often you're struck dumb, turn helpless in the face of pain. But, you notice, she says nothing and holds you too. Is this enough? It must be.

"Come," she says, and together, silently, you lay your child to rest.

At breakfast, Marta sneezes and a fine spray of blood dots the tablecloth, spawns islands of pink atop the cream. You both hesitate a second, then she snatches the pitcher and pours it out at the door. You go to hold her but she shoulders you away, clings to the frame. Beyond the stunted pole beans stands Amelia's grave, unmarked so the neighbors won't know. It's another beautiful day.

"How do you feel?" you ask, and lay a palm on her forehead. You can't tell. "You want to have Doc take a look at you?"

"What is that going to do?"

You can't answer.

"I'll try to sleep some," she says. "Maybe that'll help."

You agree hopefully, but still she doesn't turn to you, stares off at the garden as if still-hunting, looking for movement, a rabbit stealing her new shoots.

The church bell tolls a man's years. Only days ago you listened with reverence; now it's a distraction.

"Go to your work," Marta says. "You're no good around the house."

You don't have to ask what she means by this, but protest anyway.

"I'll be fine," she lies. "Go."

And, damning yourself, you do.

The bells accompany you to town. The road's busy with

millhands carrying shovels like rifles. Pickaxes, gaffs. It looks like the whole shift.

You stop John Cole, the foreman, and ask him what's happening.

"Fire's shifted east," he says.

"When'd this happen?"

"Don't know. Company wants us to dig a fire line this side of the river, run it south to the canal." He can't stop to talk, just waves and whips his stragglers on.

They pass, and suddenly no one's out. Cyril rings and rings. Town's empty again, Austin's dog blackening in the ditch. You'll get to it after you talk to Doc. Have to give Fenton his knife back at some point. Ought to be a long day.

"Leave the dog," Doc says. "It's not important. We've got to close the roads off."

"I'll have to let Bart know."

"Let him know then. I'm afraid we waited too long already."

We, he said. You don't call him on it. He knows. "How's the Colony?"

"Better than out west of town. There's a whole swamping camp there that's infected. The Colony there's a few of them sick, but Chase was smart enough to bunk them all on the top floor of the mansion. Problem is, he's got the rest of them convinced it's the Last Times."

"Pestilence," you say.

"Cleansed by a mighty fire. I figured you'd appreciate it."

"So they're waiting to be saved."

"Put it this way—I wouldn't count on them to help put it out."

Doc's always seen Chase as a fanatic. You're not so sure; you see more in him, or is it just that you want to? You don't presume.

"Who's that Cyril was ringing?"

He sighs. "Let's see. Jim Brist. Hilma Rockstad. Walter Duncan." He shakes his head. "They've been coming in at all hours. How's Amelia?"

"Not well," you say, and he nods, sorry.

"Marta?"

"The same. You send word to Irma?"

"Yep," he says. "You know she wants to come."

The two of you are quiet. You want to say you don't blame him for saving her, but you don't.

"I'll have Harlow get a wire to Bart," you say. "Then I'll set out some signs. You want anything special on them?"

"Nope. No sense everyone going crazy. Just put: 'Town Sick.' "

Across the street, Harlow's not surprised. "The number of folks I've had to notify," he says, though you both know he's sent Doc's messages to Chicago. He taps the sounder without looking, like Marta playing Bach. You ask Bart to meet you out by the town line. Please reply best time.

You tell Harlow to come get you in the cellar when Bart calls.

"How long you think we're going to be shut up?" he asks.

"However long it takes."

"You think that fire's going to wait for us? You know you can't get St. Martine anymore."

"I thought it was moving east."

"Whichever, it's headed our way, and it's not going to stop for any quarantine."

"Wait and see. It might just miss us." You thank him and walk across the street, thinking you ought to have a better answer than that. Again, you scourge yourself for not calling for a quarantine sooner. Would it make any difference? Probably not.

In the cellar, you use the cheapest white pine, knots and all. You make the signs big so they'll be readable. Slop on the whitewash, let it set, then sketch in the letters with a pencil, make sure of the spacing. Any other day, you'd let these things occupy you, lose yourself in the littlest details, but you keep thinking of the fire and how to get everyone out of town.

The line might hold, especially down by the canal.

"Nowhere else though." Once the fire gets into those oaks, it'll jump crown to crown. A few feet of dirt's not going to stop it.

The train's the simplest answer, but there's no guarantee it'll be running. By the wagonload's a possibility, but if the fire comes from the east, there's no road wide enough. You have to hope it moves west so you can send everyone to Shawano.

What about the quarantine? Bart's not going to want these people.

"Damn it," you say, feeling a sliver stick deep in your

finger. You squeeze the tip and, along with a bead of blood, the dark head pops up. Not enough. Find the tweezers right where they're supposed to be on your bench and pluck the thing out. It feels almost soft. You roll it between your fingers until it vanishes and stand there thinking maybe this is how the troubles of the world disappear when you enter the kingdom of Heaven. What does John say—this world is but a trial.

You do four, one for each main road and two to let the freight know not to pick up anyone. *S* is the hardest letter. Take your time, do it right.

Harlow comes when you're almost done and says Bart says the sooner the better.

"Tell him I'm leaving now," you say, choose a maul and take the two dryest signs up the stairs.

You ride past your house on the way out. The curtains are tied back as if nothing's wrong, and you search the windows for Marta, catch a glimpse of the crab apple in the backyard. You can only hope she's asleep, or maybe playing the melodeon with her eyes closed, filling the house with sound.

An elephant rears on the side of Ender's bridge, half-eclipsed by a new sign: USE INDIAN CORN CURE. The varnish on it smells fresh. You pass Karmann's and Weitzel's, the cut fields glinting in the heat. Their fences give way to woods; the road's rutted here, and the signs are hard to balance on your handlebars.

You slow. Beside the Hermit's lake, you turn a corner and a crow lifts off. A turtle lies crushed in the road, the track of a wheel splitting it. And there's no reason—you know the Hermit hates them, loses a precious duck to one every summer—but you stop and nudge it into the weeds.

"Getting sentimental," you say, but who are you fooling, you've always been.

Make a note to see the Hermit on the way back. Check on Marta. The firebreak. Austin's dog.

You swear for the second time today and think of Amelia. You should have listened to Marta, sent them both to Aunt Bette's. There's no sense thinking that now, but you do. You were stupid.

Still, would that have saved them or just killed Aunt Bette? You don't know.

The Hermit's lake glitters in the trees, and again you wonder how it would be to renounce everything of this world. But it's not true—he has his ducks, his cave. They say he sleeps with them on top of him like a living quilt, that he has long, odd conversations about the stars and those who would do him harm, that he preaches to the trees like some lost prophet. He's never said a word to you, only waves from across the lake to let you know he's fine, but you believe he appreciates your visits, that he thinks of you not as an intruder but as company, however brief. And you wonder if there's something kindred between you, and, yes, sometimes this worries you. To have nothing, to be beholden to no one. Maybe *this* is temptation, not Chase and his fallen women and easy prophecies. But why should you worry, you who keep to the meanest path?

Sin is in the heart. Now you would flee what you must

do, when for so long you've lorded it over others. Your goodness, your generosity. You fear that, in this, all your protestations of faith will come to nothing. You would rather be the Hermit than Chase, retire rather than have your faith tested.

"No," you protest, as if you've come to a decision.

And you have. You stand up on the pedals and ride for the line as if every second counts.

Bart's already there, stopping traffic, standing in the middle of the road, turning wagons back with his one hand. His other sleeve is neatly folded and pinned to his shoulder like a handkerchief. When you get up to him, you see his mustache is fading gray in patches, like an old dog going white around the snout. The war's been a long time gone.

"'Bout time," he says, pointing back over the drivers' heads. "What's the story?"

"Diphtheria," you say, trying to sound matter-of-fact, untouched.

"Sorry to hear it."

"Yep," you say.

"How bad? I heard Cyril ringing away this morning."

He holds the sign while you hit it with the maul, the shock rushing up your arms. You tell him most of what you know. Twenty dead, more expected. He spits in the dust in sympathy, wipes his lip with his fist. "How's old Doc holding out?"

"He's all right, just a little busy. All we need's a week or two to let things settle."

Thonk. Thonk.

"Don't think we're going to get it," he says. "That fire's not taking the stage. Got everyone riled up over here. They're running around like a bunch of dumb hens. Half of town's cleared out and the other half's stocked up on buckets."

"You got a fire line started?"

"Done," he says. "It won't hold. It's like drawing a mark on the levee and telling the river she can't rise."

You wiggle the sign, give it another whack. The post splits, a long splinter dangling. "Cheap pine."

"Does the job," Bart says.

A man you half-recognize stops his buckboard and calls over, "How long?"

Bart shrugs. "Long as it takes. It's up to Jake here."

It's what they called you in the army. Like you, Bart can't quite give up that life.

"How long?" the man demands.

"A week," you guess, "maybe longer. Why?"

"I got business at the mill."

"Sorry about that."

"I come all the way from Sheboygan. I got fifty pair of good boots here."

"Might try and wire," Bart suggests. "You could leave the boots here and have someone come get 'em."

The man swears, and you want to tell him his fifty boots don't mean a thing, that he's not looking at the situation correctly. Instead you ask him to turn around so other folks can get by. He doesn't argue, just sneers and flips his reins, wheels around so his dust rolls over you.

"Idjit," Bart says.

There are more. The two of you stand there, Bart with his arm across his stomach, yours crossed, the maul still in one hand, as if guarding the sign. You field the same questions, almost start to believe your answers. The last wagon rolls off and the road's clear.

"All right," you say. "No one in, no one out."

"I'll do my best," Bart says, though you both know you're too busy to watch it all the time. You never saw the paper man for the circus or INDIAN CORN CURE; they come through at night.

You start to move off, but Bart calls you back.

"What if the fire comes while you're still sick?"

All your half-made plans rise up in your mind and then fall, lie down like scythed hay.

"No one in, no one out."

"No matter what," Bart says, giving you one last chance.

"No matter what," you say, and give him a look to make sure he understands. It catches him off-guard, that look, too hard, part of a long-gone war. But it can't be too hard for what you're saying, and again you wonder if this is Amelia.

His lips part. He doesn't take his eyes off you, as if you've drawn on him and it's his play.

"All right," he says, but you wonder if he really believes it.

You pound the other one into the ground far enough off the track so it doesn't get run over. The canal cuts through here, arrow straight, its limestone walls bright, the water low and black as grease, cottonwood fluff sprinkled across the top, and clumps of fat waterlilies. On the towpath a scattering of dung draws flies. Your sign can be seen by the drovers, lets them know to keep going south, to not take on cargo. You knot the maul to a belt loop and walk your bike back through the crackling weeds to the road and head back toward town.

Even this far out you can hear Cyril ringing the hour—three. Everything seems to be taking too long today.

You've promised yourself to look in on the Hermit, so at the bend in the road you hop off and pad through the shadows and across the soft pine duff until it turns marshy and the light off the water is blinding. On the far shore, his ducks mill and rip at the grass outside the cave mouth. Must be twenty of them by now, he has a talent for them sure. They say he believes people want to poison them, that he guards them like a mother. You shield your eyes and try to find him, that rick of rags and matted hair.

"Ho!" you cry, and wave your arms over your head, looking for movement. "Ho there!"

You hope he's in. Sometimes in summer they say he takes off for the hills. Too many folks in the woods for his taste. Children pester him, and young people out picnicking. You too?

"Ho! Ho there!"

The ducks pay no mind to you, pluck up the grass. You wonder if you should walk around the near end and see if he's all right. You have to check on Marta. Austin's dog.

"Hell's bells," you say, just as you see him emerge from the cave.

He's wearing the yellow shirt you left for him this spring, and it looks like he's trimmed his beard. You're pleased with how presentable he is, as if it's your doing. You wave and he waves back, a tiny figure beneath the dry pines, and you realize he needs to know about the fire. You cross your arms over your head and wave them back and forth.

He does the same.

You wait, wondering if he understands, then do it again.

He repeats it.

"No," you say, then cup your hands around your mouth and holler, "fire." It echoes.

He shakes his head.

Holler it again.

Nothing.

You point to the near end of the lake and start walking along the shore, and soon he does too.

You meet at a rippling spillway ruled by a wide beaver dam. Closer, you can see the ragged cut of his beard. Probably used an old knife whetted on soft limestone. His hair's nearly white all over, and a knee pokes out of his dungarees. He walks hunched, head bent, like he's still in the cave.

"There's a fire coming," you call across the gap.

"Eh?"

"I said, there's a fire coming."

"I can't hear so good," he says, and pats his ears. "Took sick this winter."

You walk out on the dam, feeling it gently give under your boots. He climbs his side easily, in wide strides, making you aware of how town you are. Even before you lean across the spillway, you can smell the stink of infection. His fingernails are so long they're curled like ram's horns. He turns his ear to hear you. And still, inches apart, you're separated, part of the world and not.

"There's a fire coming. Big one. Killed a bunch of Winnebagos up north."

He nods to let you know he heard you, but doesn't say anything.

"You gonna be all right out here?"

He nods. "I got the lake."

"You'll jump in when it comes. Think of yourself. Don't go running around after those ducks."

Nods again. He looks off at the water, lost.

"All right," you say. "Just thought you ought to know."

"Right obliged," he says, and turns and tromps away over the dam like it's a sidewalk, his long hair swinging, and you realize what you can give him, how you can help.

"Hold on there," you call, and when he turns to see what you want, you already have the knife out, its pretty finish catching the sun.

He climbs the dam to you, looks but doesn't take it. "Already got one."

"Always use another."

"That's true," he says, and takes it, weighs it in his hand. "That is true."

There's no one out west of town, the bogs shimmering in the heat. The Endeavor road's empty all the way to the line, and as you roll past the houses, you remember what Doc said about the swamping camp and wonder about the people inside, behind the windows and old horsehair screens. Millie and Elsa's yard is burnt brown, the roses withered, the fence still busted up. The roadway's baked, and driving the sign in raises a sweat. There's no fire line out here, and everything's brittle as tinder.

Do the railroad in the stink of creosote. No time to climb up Cobb's tunnel, though you suspect you'd find a nice breeze on top. Get it done, get going.

Marta's asleep when you check on her, in bed, her shift and stockings hung over the commode. She breathes so shallowly, a long pause in between, and you wonder if Doc could help any. Probably not. It's not his fault. Chase can't save them either, nurses, mansion, fancy city medicine and all. The only cure is to wait, have faith, hold to what's your own. When isn't that so?

You look at her face and see Amelia's, the sudden upturn at the corner of her lips, the smile she wears when she's not even trying, and then you're on your knees again, asking Him to be merciful this time, to care for those who are His. It's selfish, this beseeching, but there's nothing without her, you've already lost Amelia, a man can only bear so much.

Abraham and Isaac. Lot. Job. These are all lessons you've preached, yet when it comes time to walk in their shoes you run from it.

"Who wouldn't?" you ask, and before standing up, you kneel there a moment in the whiskey-colored light, motes rising up between you and the window giving on the backyard, and find you can't answer that question. A month ago you would have said—with no hesitation—any good Christian, but now you pull yourself up, careful not to wake Marta, grab your hat and head out the door, completely silent.

Austin's dog is a mess—black with flies and mushy in the guts. It breaks in two when you lift it with a shovel. You're used to the stink, but something about it makes you angry, and after you shovel dust over the hole, you bang the blade against a tree, tearing off a chunk of bark, and, suddenly stricken, you bend and find the missing piece and try to fit it back on. It doesn't stick, and savagely you kick the trunk. Pick up the shovel and head back toward the churchyard. It's hot. Maybe you're crazed like Marta was last night, maybe that's it.

"Crazy Jacob the Undertaker," you say.

But when you reach the churchyard you shut up. Don't want to be seen muttering among the tombstones, no. Then you realize the boys who make fun of you aren't around now.

Look around town. Fenton's never opened. The livery's shut up, and Ritter's. You and Doc are the only ones. Even the mill's off digging ditches.

Cyril breaks you out of the spell, ringing six. Supper-time. No wonder everyone's gone. You're the only one not home.

And why not?

You decide to look in on Doc, see how things are with him, but there's a sign in his window: VISITING.

Walk along the picket fences, smell the chicken fricassee, the boiled corn, the steaming crusts of pies. You expect to meet someone straggling back from the fire line, or a family moving through with their furniture piled high in the back of a wagon, but there's nothing. Crickets. The rustle of a jay lifting out of a rose bush. Under the oaks, the air goes cool, and you see Mrs. Bagwell lift her shade and take you in, then let it drop again. Another day you'd wave, but you walk along as if you haven't seen her.

Your door's locked. Inside, it's silent, and you don't call for Marta. She's still in bed, and while you're standing there, she coughs, hard, her body jerking under the covers. Her bangs are plastered to her forehead. Bend and press the back of your hand to her skin. Burning. Fever sleep. You want to wake her up and ask her what you're supposed to do.

What did she do with Amelia?

Waited. Attended her.

Yes, but that didn't work.

You want to run back to town and ask Doc, but he's not there, he's out helping someone else.

For a minute you stand there, stuck, unsure, then go into the kitchen and paw through the larder. A half rasher of bacon, some potatoes. You dig a few splits of stovewood from the bin and get them going, lay the bacon in a skillet. When the fat turns gray you flip it and start chopping the potatoes. Take your jacket off, it's too hot. Get the whole mess cooking, the grease washing over everything. Not elegant, but it's all the army taught you.

"Not all," you say, seeing the dark of those nights.

You look in on her before sitting down to the table. Still asleep, breathing.

You say grace with your hands clasped above your plate.

It's awful, sodden with grease, and after a few bites you quit. Eat the bacon with your fingers, remembering the bloody strips of flesh, the cries in the night.

Drop it on the plate. Dump the plate in the scrap bucket. There's whiskey in the cupboard; the root cellar's full of hard cider and ginger beer.

You walk through the rooms of the house. The empty crib sends you to the backyard. The crab apple bows. The sun's going down and it's all in shadow, and you kneel there like a man checking on his garden, inspecting the leaves for chinch bugs. The dirt in the corner is dried and cracked, an ant struggling across it, carrying another ant bent double. Glance over the fences on both sides; there's no one. You press your hand to the cool earth as if spreading it on her chest, close your eyes.

What do you see when you remember her? Marta bathing her in the tub, a hand cupping her head. Playing on the floor, holding her above you and watching her tiny feet kick. Her one tooth.

She never said a word.

Open your eyes and it seems darker, dusk settling above the oaks. Bats flap, or are those swallows?

Stand up and go inside, light the lamp. Think of whiskey, then dismiss it. You've seen enough drunken fools make a mess of the cell, then wake the next day cradling their heads.

You go in to Marta, go get the rocker from the nursery and sit there in the dark, listening. Close your eyes. Notice how it's never totally quiet, how the very air seems to have a sound. Or is that you? When she wakes up, you think, she'll be hungry.

Not with a fever.

"When the fever breaks," you say.

It didn't break with Amelia. Why should it break with her?

Because she's older, grown.

So was Lydia Flynn.

You don't know why. It will. Have faith.

Those nights in Kentucky, you promised Him everything. Just get me through this and the rest of my life is Yours. You could hear the Rebs calling across the water, taunting, and the little Norwegian beside you coughing. He'd been weak since the beginning, riddled with consumption, and you kept him alive, fed him that horse piece by filthy piece till you stripped it to the hooves. And still the shells tore over, sent rocks and clods of mud from the cliffs thumping down around you. You scratched the days into the dirt like a prisoner till you snapped your knife trying to pry the meat out of a knee joint like an oyster. You remember the captain calling roll in the dark, and the scattered responses, less every night. And then he stopped calling. The water ran by, high from the rains. The Reb fires popped on the far shore. Laughter, a fiddle scratching.

A mouse scuttles in the kitchen, and you open your eyes. Darkness. Marta. How long have you been sitting here?

Check your watch. She's still asleep—probably best for her. Tomorrow you've got a lot to do. Go into the sitting room and blow out the lamp.

Get in beside her. She's hot from being under the feather tick all day. Kiss her cheek and lie back and read the ceiling. Wonder how the fire line's going, if it's reached the canal. Old Meyer out there on the Shawano road, alone.

You know you won't sleep.

Why don't you pray?

You already have.

Who would have thought you'd turn bitter? Of all people.

And so you roll over and whisper another prayer into your pillow. Not because you're too proud to admit you're wrong. Not because you're afraid. Because you can't change who you are.

Cyril rings eight people the next day. The fire moves to the west. Marta sleeps in her fever. You touch a wet cloth to her lips, lay it on her forehead. She doesn't stir, only a delicate pulse at her neck, the blue lump of a vein. A hard crab apple has fallen on Amelia's grave. You gouge it with a fingernail, then pitch it into the bushes. Make beans and bacon for yourself, have a ginger beer. When you check on Marta, you purposely don't look too close. Why? Won't your faith save you?

The next morning you go to see how Old Meyer's holding out and find everyone dead—or Old Meyer and Marcus. Shotgun, looks like. Meyer's inside, half his head gone, his pipe still neatly balanced on the table. You search the house and then the outbuildings, finally come on Marcus in the barn, in the sleigh, the tarpaulin thrown back, stippled with holes. Probably trying to hide. The others are down by the hives, the crosses neatly done, and you take a good portion of the morning to lay their father and brother beside them. Mark them too, bless them.

Doc says he doesn't see another way out of it, you'll have to burn the house down.

"I figured," you say, so he knows the decision's not just his. He's the first person you've talked to today, and it's a relief.

"How's Amelia?" he asks, and you answer him with a lie.

"I'm glad," he says, and you're glad he doesn't ask about Marta. "I think we got the road closed just in time."

You mention the fire turning back west and he rubs his mustache with a thumb—first one wing, then the other.

"How long's the quarantine going to be?" you ask, like everyone else.

"Two weeks to do any good."

"Two weeks."

"One week at the least. It takes five days to incubate. Less in children. If we enforce quarantine house by house, a week might do it, but that means nobody goes outside."

You bring up the fire line, the shift from the mill. There's no place they can all bunk together. And they have family, most of them. No, he's got to come up with something better.

"Here," Doc says. "If the fire comes, it comes. Nothing I can do about it."

"I'm not arguing with you."

"I'm doing the best I can," he says, "but there are just too many of them. And even if it was just one or two, there's not much I can do for them. Do you understand me?"

"I understand," you say, and think of the valise in the front hall closet. "We're in the same boat here."

"I know you know, Jacob," he says, and yawns hard, rubs his face with both hands so it goes red. "It's just hard to watch it happen."

He's right, and you agree, but on the Shawano road, in the killing heat, you get to thinking about Irma waiting for him and it's different.

When blood goes cold it sticks to what it touches, stains like red clay. You had to scrub the tub in the backyard, pour the water into the garden.

You've brought a jug of kerosene, in case, but end up using Meyer's. Slosh it over the chairs and through the kitchen, a bandanna over your face so the fumes don't choke you. It's calm, but still you worry about the grass catching, back away after tossing the spunk on the rug.

For a second you think it's gone out, then a breath of white smoke like steam leaks out the door, a flame jumps in a window, cracks it, and soon a black billowing cloud rolls skyward and fire knifes through the roof. You close the gate and stand by the road, watching Meyer's place burn. His family and all his hard work, come to nothing. If he did go through that soldier's pockets, what is that compared to this? Everything's been stolen from him, and you did nothing to stop it.

"It's not right," you say.

Who are you angry with?

Not God.

No? Who else is there? Is this the devil's work?

It must be, you think, but uncertainly. It must be, but you're confused.

Maybe tonight you'll sleep.

"Maybe."

But you don't. You hold on to Marta, warming her with your own body, listening, imagining her breathing.

Cyril rings and rings. You want to climb the ladder and silence him, beg him to stop. You arrange the comforter over Marta, kiss her before you leave. You need food, and there's laundry to do.

Town's quiet. Town's always quiet now. The dogs keep you busy. You find them behind the livery, alongside the churchyard, in the middle of the road. You toss them in the brush with Austin's, shovel dust over the pile to keep the flies off.

It's like the war again.

Burn down houses. Burn down barns filled with dead cattle, coops filled with chickens.

At Bjornsons, one hen isn't dead and tries to fly, its feathers burning. You hit it with your shovel until it stops.

"Sorry," you say, even though no one's around, only the Bjornsons laid out by the woodpile, waiting for you to take care of them. Emil was more afraid of the fire.

"I am too," you say. "Still, better west than east."

Crazy Jacob.

"Fiddlesticks," you say, and take up the shovel again, bend your back. Dig them deep enough so the coyotes don't get them.

At home you learn to make cornbread from a recipe. Marta's writing goes all over the place.

"Is this salt?" you ask.

What else would it be?

"I don't know," you say.

Two teaspoons of salt.

"I've never made this before."

Don't fret, it'll be fine. Take a rest while it rises. Come in here and sit with us.

Marta's on the love seat in the blue dress you like, Amelia in her lap. You bring your whiskey in and sit with them. In the kitchen the stove hisses, a knot pops. You put your arm around her, give her a kiss on her cool, rouged cheek.

"How are you feeling?"

Much better. It must have been the sleep.

"And how about you?" you say, and pick up Amelia, lift her under the arms so her feet dangle. Her blue, blue eyes.

You give her a kiss and return her to Marta, get up to check on your cornbread, but at the doorway you turn back to look at them, to admire them sitting there, the ones you love, and count yourself lucky, yes, even blessed, having almost lost them.

6

All morning the quarantine brings town out of their houses. To challenge it, to complain of the decision, dispute its usefulness, its legality. They come to you with questions you can't answer, though out of politeness—out of duty—you try. Byron Merrill, Bill Tilton—people you haven't seen in weeks. They crowd into the jail, clog the sidewalk. They've already been to Doc, they say; like children polling their parents, they're hoping you'll give them a different answer, make an exception to the rule.

"We're all in the same boat," you say, knowing it won't placate them.

How long, they all want to know.

"One week, maybe two."

"What are we supposed to do till then?" Fenton says. "I've got business to tend to."

"Then tend to it," you say.

"How am I supposed to do that? I've got a shipment of coffee sitting in Shawano I can't get to."

"Have them ship it."

It'll cost too much to ship.

Mrs. Bagwell's daughter is stuck in Shawano.

Carl Huebner was off on business, and now he can't get back in.

And George Peck, down to Rockford buying brick for the mill.

Why can't they come in if they want to? It's their risk, no one else's. Long as no one's going out, what's the difference?

"It's for the good of everyone," you say, as if logic might satisfy them. You want to say it's not your fault, yet a week ago you were ready to close the roads. Which is it?

"I see you got Marta and your daughter all nice and locked up," Mrs. Bagwell accuses. "Taking no chances with them."

"No," you say, "and I'd suggest you do the same."

"That's no kind of advice," Fenton says.

You turn on him, shoulders squared, like you mean to fight, then stop yourself. "It's the right thing and you know it." Then to everyone: "Two weeks is not a long time."

Grumbling, an obscenity that—admit it—shocks you. No one believes you. Two weeks is a lifetime.

"Go on," you say, "I've got my own work," and herd them out, waving your hat around like they're cattle.

You're right, you think, it is the right thing. Why do you have to justify it?

Not all of them leave you alone. Emmett Nelligan won't

let go of his sister Esther coming to visit. She came all the way from Ohio just to have Bart stop her at the line. She's in a boardinghouse in Shawano, terrified; she doesn't know anyone there.

You try to ignore him, collect everything from your desk before you leave. You need to wire Bart, check the fire line, look in on Doc.

"Every day it's costing money to put her up," he says.

You stop and look at him. "You don't honestly want her in the middle of all this, do you?"

"I'm not sick," he argues. "I can't see what harm it would do—"

"Don't," you say. "There's no point in it."

"I don't want her to be alone there," he says, and what can you say but you're sorry? You understand him completely.

Go over the telegraph office and have Harlow tell Bart that everyone's unhappy. Phrased that way, it makes sense. They don't hate you, they're just frustrated. Deep down, they understand it's best for everyone. They must.

Bart thinks differently; he expects some of them to make a break for it. He has a deputy posted by the sign, making sure everyone's on the right side. It's costing him fifty cents a day, but he knows you don't have time. You've promised to help him as much as you can, and with every minute you spend away from the line, you feel more and more obliged.

Harlow's swamped. Doc says it's fine for you to bring

mail in, but no outgoing post, so Harlow's got a mess of wires to send. His bottom lip is black where he's licked his quill. His hands ride the keys like spiders.

"Get St. Martine back yet?"

"Nope," he says, concentrating, then relaxes, lifts his hands. "I tried Madison this morning and couldn't get through. Tried to bypass through Milwaukee and that's as far as I got. Everything north of here's dead."

"How about west?"

"I can get Montello, if that's what you mean."

"West of that?"

"Everything's fine that way, but there's nothing out there. Montello's the one you're worried about."

"Can't fool you," you say.

"Don't worry, I'll let you know as soon as she goes."

"Think she will now?"

"Tell the truth," he says, "I'm surprised she's still up."

Out on the fire line, John Cole has his crew almost to the canal. Their picks fall in rhythm like a railroad gang. You're not surprised by their bandannas. With the pale dust rising around them, and the long, broad trench, they look like gravediggers after a battle.

"They say it's headed west again," you tell John.

"So are we when we're finished here."

"Use the river."

"Hitch it to that stretch of road this side of Cobb's." He says it like it's not his idea, waits for you to suggest a better one, and you know why. The road goes east-west; even if the fire doesn't jump the line, it can stick to one side and run right into town. There's nothing but woods out there, a few grassy pastures.

"Not much else you *can* do," you say.

"Nope," he agrees glumly, and goes off to show the crew how close to the tracks they can dig.

Hiking back through the thicket, you notice deadfall parceled around the living trees like tinder. Even the jack pine are drying up, tufted with clumps of orange needles. You can afford to ignore the planks laid across low spots; the ground's hard, the ferns withered. When you get to the road, you search the sky like a farmer. The high blue stretches for Iowa.

Bart's deputy's name is Millard—just a boy growing too fast for his clothes. He paces the line, holds a rifle like a soldier, solemn as Jeff Davis himself. Bart's taught him well. Far off, Cyril rings three.

"All quiet?" you ask, and as Millard says, "Yessir," the two of you hear the same jingling music and turn to see a procession coming up the road.

It's the circus—red wagons and pennants flying. An elephant raises dust like a column on the march.

"Oh my gosh," Millard says, forgetting his charge. "Oh my gosh!"

You've never seen one either, and watch it come on, interested in the way its skin moves, the funny trunk, the ridiculous ears, the dainty tail. You see why people called heading into battle Going to See the Elephant. No one could describe this to you, you have to see it for yourself.

A huge orchestrion on its own wagon thumps a tune. The horses' bits are silvered, their heads plumed. They have big cats in gilded cages, leashed bear cubs tussling, a man handling a snake as thick as your leg. As they approach, you naturally step aside in deference, then remember and go out to meet them, a hand in the air.

The man driving the first wagon wears spectacles and a striped vest, like a chemist. He hauls on the reins and the team stops short. You can smell their horrible breath, their legs wetted against the heat.

"What is it, neighbor?" the driver asks.

"Town's quarantined. We can't let you in."

"What have you got?"

"Diphtheria."

He thinks on this, as if weighing their chances. "All we want's to pass on through. We won't so much as step down, any of us."

"Can't let you."

"We can do it at a trot," he says. "Won't take but five minutes."

You apologize but it's not possible.

"Well, Goddamn you then," he says pleasantly, and stands up on the bench to fish in a pocket. He pulls out a five-dollar bill and tries to hand it to you.

You look at it, then at him. The orchestrion goes on. "You'll have to loop around south. There's wildfire north of here."

"Five minutes," he tries again. "Down south's going to take us way out of our way. We need to be in Montello—"

"You're not listening to me," you say, and find you've grabbed his wrist to pull him closer, and you see he's afraid, that you're hurting him. You twist his arm and he winces, shifts his body to accommodate it. "If you cross that line I will have to kill you, and I will. People are dying here. If you want to be one of them, then come on. Otherwise, you leave us be."

He takes his arm back warily, then starts to turn his wagon around, bumping over the lip of the road.

"South," you call after him, but he doesn't look back. The other drivers fix you with a glare, which you return expertly, daring them to say a word, spit, anything. None of them do, except the elephant, who leaves a single cannonball of a dropping as he swings around; it raises a puff of dust, then sits there like an insult as the tinny music fades.

Millard gapes at it, amazed. "Why," he says, "that thing's as big as my head."

You laugh at him, but wonder why you threatened the man, what made you do it.

It's everything, you think. It's reasonable, considering, but still you ask forgiveness, promise to stay on guard against your temper.

"I would of liked to see it," Millard says. "The circus."

"You saw more than most," you say, and because of who you are, he agrees.

Nobody in, nobody out.

"I don't want you shooting anyone though," you tell him. "That's up to me and Sheriff Cox. If it comes to that, shoot straight in the air."

"But the sheriff said—"

"I know what he said. I'll have a talk with him, don't you worry."

He seems deflated, and to soothe him you show him the army way to about-face, how to pivot just one heel, use the other toe to bring you clean around. You leave him practicing, counting cadence to himself, walking box-guard around the dropping.

Riding, you shake your head at Bart. Have to talk to him, get someone with a little more hair on his chin.

In town, another crew's wetting down the roof of the mill with a hose, drenching the mounds of cast-off sapwood. Lumber's piling up because of the quarantine. The hose is anchored in the river, and two big Swedes are working the water engine like a teeter-totter. The channel's narrow; on the cracked flats the sun's baking a stranded sucker. You'll have to set out barrels of sand at each street corner, find enough buckets. At least there's no chance of panicking anyone further.

Tomorrow, though. There's hardly anything left of today. You didn't even get lunch. Too much to do.

You stop in at Doc's before closing up shop. He's got a list of families you need to keep an eye on, and two bodies he wants you to get to before you go home.

"Who?" you ask.

"May Blanton and little Stevie Roy."

You wish you were still shocked, that you'd search for a reason these two were taken. May's only a few years older than you, and Stevie's almost ten, resentful that people still call him "little." Someone like Elsa Sullivan you expect to die, not these two.

"I've got both houses under quarantine," Doc says. "It's coming to that, specially west of town. Tomorrow I'd appreciate it if you'd come with me to look in on some folks. They don't tend to like what I have to tell them. And some are sure to have family that need to be taken care of. I'd like you to bury them on their land, where it's possible. These two can go in the churchyard if they'll fit."

"I'll fit them," you say, and it feels good, after so long, to make a promise you know you can keep.

"And don't bleed them," he says. "Do I have to tell you that?"

"No," you say, and this time you mean it.

To make up for it, you do good work on their coffins; don't skimp, dig their plots deep. It's good to work, to feel the hurt in your shoulders, your forearms hard. Grunt, blow a drop of sweat off your nose. You almost don't think of Amelia, the spot in the garden. No, they're both at home, safe, waiting for you. There's no way they can get it; you've told them not to go out, to lock the door. You'll protect them, keep them secret.

It's night by the time you pack the dirt flat with your boots, and when you go to close up the jail, you find someone has smeared your door with dung.

At first you think of the elephant, and Millard, but without sniffing you can tell this is horse. You go inside and find an old *County Record* to swab it off with.

"Fenton," you say.

Emmett Nelligan.

Strange to admit, it could be anyone. Suddenly Friendship's a nest of enemies.

Just frustrated.

No, more. You think of the circus driver's eyes, the way he understood what you were capable of.

You finish daubing it off, but there's nowhere to throw the paper away. You look up and down the street, then cross and stuff it under Fenton's sidewalk, rinse your hands in the scummy trough water.

Marta's waiting for you in the dark with Amelia. You light the lamp and visit with them, then go into the kitchen and make dinner. Beans and fatback tonight, the captain's favorite.

Set the table, arrange everyone around it—Amelia in her high chair, Marta right beside her. Say grace.

After dinner Marta plays the melodeon and the two of you sing. She falls off the stool but you prop her up, set her feet on the pedals, her fingers on the keys, help her find middle C. *Jesus Our Redeemer. He Will Come in Glory for Me.* Amelia plays on the floor with her cornhusk doll.

And then it's late, time for bed. The two of you tuck Amelia in, then retire. You read a section of Mrs. Stowe to Marta. Finish, but she's asleep, far gone, the plain of her cheek turned to you, and you kiss her tenderly, hold her to you, careful not to wake her.

Friday's the same—Millard on guard, everyone with questions. You ride beside Doc out west of town and stop at the quarantine houses. In the back of the wagon is a bucket of whitewash, and while Doc is inside with the Ramsays and Doles and Schnackmeiers, you paint a shaky *Q* on their front doors. Leave the bucket on the porch and join them, explain the legal consequences of breaking quarantine. The fathers nod solemnly, the mothers fix you with their eyes, sick with the idea that you would do this to decent people. Doc apologizes, says there's no other way, that there are lots of folks in the same shape.

And then the tour of the sickroom, masks over your faces as Doc bends to the infected. The mother comes with you, but no one else, stands behind you like a guide to the underworld. A lamp burns, the windows are closed. Under the comforter, the children sweat.

Sarah Ramsay has already lost two of the four boys—Martin and Gavin. You've always thought of them as mean, even evil children, and now, ashamed, forgive them everything. Just wild boys, high-spirited. Across the small room from the living, the dead lie in bed together.

"Would you like Jacob to see to them?" Doc offers.

"No thank you," she says, so calmly that after checking Tyrone's throat he asks her again.

"Oh, no thank you."

The *Q* on their door runs, white tendrils reaching for the floor. Hang a sign on the gate so no one stops.

"It won't be long there," Doc says.

"What about her?" you ask.

He doesn't have an answer, just flips his ledger, finds the next name on the page.

The whole road, no exceptions.

"Why do you think that is?" you ask. "Why's it worse out here than in town?"

"Threshing," he guesses. "People in town don't help each other. They stay inside. I don't know, any number of reasons."

You chew on this as you bump along. First the soldier in the woods, then Lydia Flynn. Clytie. You think if you solve the mystery of how it got here that you can somehow reverse the process, make everybody well again. It's pointless, but you fit the clues together. The soldier slept in Elsa and Millie's barn. Lydia Flynn entertained him in a back pasture at the Colony. Everything you come up with is missing a beginning. Who had it first? Where did it come from?

At Heilemanns, no one answers the door. Doc thumps it with a fist, but still no one comes.

"Constable," you holler. "Frank, Katie, you in there?"

The front's locked, the blinds drawn, and you walk around back. It's locked too, but you find a pry bar in the dovecote and let yourself in, calling through the darkened rooms.

The parlor's neat, the beds empty. Upstairs there's a cat basking on a windowsill; it mews when it sees you, slinks over to rub against your boots.

"Don't touch it," Doc says, and you straighten up, pull back your hand.

The dust in the attic is undisturbed, an unbroken coating.

You expect to find them hanging in the woodshed, or in the well house, throats gashed open with sheep shears, by the milk house, drowned, their heads stuck in the rain barrel. There's nothing; the doors open on cordwood, baled hay, cobwebs.

"You been talking with Montello at all?" Doc asks.

"Yes," you say, and you have, though nowhere near as often as you've talked to Bart. You should have someone watching the road out where the valley narrows by Cobb's tunnel. You'll wire up the line, give them a description.

"May be too late now," Doc says.

"I'll do what I can," you say, and feel betrayed. Heilemanns were good church people. Frank sang bass, Katie made a fine strawberry pie. What could it be but a lack of faith? That's partly your fault.

The children were sick, so the house has to go.

"You want to take care of that cat before you fire it," Doc says.

"Way it's been so dry, I can't burn it till I get a crew."

"Then get the cat now."

"It can't wait?"

"Jacob," he says, and you see he means it. Climbing the stairs, you wonder if it's the disease that's changed him, the demands on his skill, and think it must be. He's not heartless. These people are his flock too, his responsibility. He's lost almost as much as you have.

You tug your gloves on. "Here, puss," you call, and make kissing sounds with your lips. "Here, puss-puss."

You kill it like a chicken, with a twist. Its claws catch on the gloves' rawhide. All the muscles stop at once, and again you marvel at God's invention, His intricacy. You lay the cat on the sill, turn its head around so it seems to be sunning, just as you found it.

In the buckboard, Doc thanks you.

"Who's next?" you say, hard, then want to apologize; you're not angry with him.

Millie and Elsa's house needs burning, and Terfel's sheep are spread over a meadow, moldering in the heat. You visit the sick until the sun touches the trees. The whitewash is almost gone.

"Have to get a party out tomorrow," Doc says on the way back, and though tomorrow's Saturday, you agree. You'll talk to John Cole, ask for his best men; they should be out west of town anyhow.

"What else can we do?" you ask.

"Just keep them inside," Doc says. "Make sure none of them go the way of Heilemanns. That's when you get an epidemic, when people start running off in the middle of the night."

Back at the jail, Harlow's left a packet of wires marked *Undeliverable*, meaning the addressee is either dead or quarantined. Break the bundle into two stacks, nearly equal. You try not to read them, but you know they're from family, that every message is urgent.

First thing tomorrow, you think, and snuff the lamp. Even you're turning heartless. Just tired, you argue, but unconvincingly.

Locking your door, you smell dung, but it's just a pile

left by Doc's team. Probably where the disease comes from. Damn horses.

For supper it's cabbage soup and a heel of bread. Got to stop in Fenton's and pick something up.

"What an awful day," you say, and tell Marta all about it. Amelia looks at you slightly cross-eyed. The soup is thin and bitter, and you pitch it in the bushes, stand out in the backyard looking at the stars, the dish in your hand. Later, under the covers, Marta's skin warms to yours, and you lay there with your arms around her, reciting prayers enough for all of Friendship.

Up early and out of the house, to deliver Harlow's messages. You expect people to be grateful, pleased to hear from loved ones, but none of them speak to you until Margaret Kyne says, "And how am I supposed to wire her back? You just said yesterday I can't leave this house."

"I'll have Harlow send it for you," you offer, and she slams the door. You wait for her to come back, thinking she's inside, writing. She doesn't.

John lends you some of his crew, and you fire Millie and Elsa's, the roses going up with the porch, tin roof buckling thunderously. After lunch you do two more. At Heilemanns, the cat's where you left it, its eyes milky. The men seem to understand, dig the fire line with the same patience they'd tend the blades at the mill. You slosh the drapes with kerosene, darken the carpet, then stand in the drive with the rest of them, watching the flames eat down to the chimneys.

"Takes longer 'n I thought," Kip Cheyney says, and a few of you agree.

Millard says a drummer with a valise full of patent medicines tried to bribe him and that Bart said he could fire at will.

"Where *is* Sheriff Cox?" you ask, and he takes a step back, gives you the same face the circus driver had. "I will talk to him," you say. "Meantime I do not want you shooting anybody."

You interrupt Harlow and tell him to tell Bart that Millard is wrong for the job and to get someone on there who's done some killing cause it might just come to that.

"That true?" Harlow asks.

"Would I say it if it wasn't?" you say, and leave him to his keys.

Not halfway across the street and you see your window's busted. Inside, there's glass on the floor, and a rock; it's taken a gouge out of your desk. You investigate, then come back out, look around Main Street and roll the rock under the sidewalk. Rub your thumb over the gouge; it won't smooth away.

"Goddamn," you say, disappointed in them. You're just doing what's best for everyone, don't they know that?

Tomorrow's Sunday and you haven't even thought of a sermon.

Am I my brother's keeper?

It's a start.

No one's going to be there.

I will.

No one else though.

Doesn't matter.

Saturday is bath night, and after a supper of just beans, you pull the tub out and put the kettle on. Getting Marta out of her blue dress, you decide you need to do laundry. The bottoms of her arms are turning purple, and scrubbing does nothing. Work the lather into her hair. Do the hard-to-get spots first—the back of the neck, under the breasts, behind the knees. A second kettle to rinse. Check the water with your wrist, not too hot. You want to think the heat brings a bloom to her cheek, but it doesn't. Still, her skin's warm. Towel her down, fluff up her hair, brush it in the mirror. Then a nightshirt and into new, clean sheets.

Pour another kettle and ease in, strip the soot off your arms, the smoke out of your hair. You're faster than Marta, and when you get in bed, it's still warm. You take her hand and pull her to you, and she lays her head on your chest. The clean smell of her hair reminds you of courting, how she'd lean back against you in the swing and let you hold her. You do that now and close your eyes, and today is over, gone and done with, and you're with her again.

Cyril wakes you, banging out the dead. In church, he's the only one. He sits in his usual spot in the back, smack in the middle of the pew, as if the other parishioners might suddenly show up. And still, you appreciate his loyalty. The Lord *does* provide for His children. We *are* all blessed, even the least of us. You pick Abraham and Isaac—an old favorite—and preach to him as if he's a crowd, a whole town.

Midafternoon, Sarah Ramsay wanders into town, wild-eyed, her apron covered in blood, her nose still pumping out gouts. Her mouth opens as if to scream, but nothing comes out.

You collar her, steer her into Doc's office.

"They're all, dead," she squeezes out, rocking. "My boys."

"Jacob here will take care of them," Doc says, trying to soothe her, but she doesn't stop. He tidies her up as best he can. "Here," he says to you, "go look after them and I'll be out with her directly."

On the road, you swear you smell smoke, though you can't see anything. Have to check with Harlow and see what Montello has to say.

You find the Ramsays two to a bed, just like last time, still in their nightshirts. Find a shady place by the wood-line. You try Martin first but his bare legs bother you, and you have to find some dungarees for him. The others too, all four of them nestled against each other, the dirt tucked up to their chins like covers. The dust powders their hair, sticks to their lips, and then they're gone.

Doc brings Sarah Ramsay out in the buckboard. She's wearing a dowdy housedress of Irma's, one nostril plugged with cotton. He steadies her across the backyard to show her your work. She stares at the mound, dry-eyed, stunned, like a trout struck by an osprey and left to gasp in the shallows. She turns to thank you, but can only mouth the words, her voice a squeak.

"I'm very sorry," you say, and pat her on the shoulder, a professional touch Mr. Simmons drilled into you. Make contact. Be a friend to the bereaved. Why does it sound false now?

The *Q* on the front door's already cracking. It's sloppy work, which stings you. Doc leads Sarah Ramsay inside and sits her down in the parlor on an old sofa while you stand at the door like a footman.

"I want you to rest," he says. "I'll look in on you tomorrow."

She nods, defeated, but later that afternoon she comes stumbling into town, mute and bloody, and Doc has you board up the windows, put a lock on the door. It's best, he says. There's nothing anyone can do; at least this will keep other people safe. You don't believe any of it, though you know he's talking sense. You drive the nails cleanly, make sure the space between the boards is too small to crawl through.

She understands when she sees it. She scratches and spits, tries to bite you. It takes both of you to push her in, ripping Irma's housedress in the process. She screams nothing, showing her teeth. Shoulder it closed. She breaks the windows all around the house. Crashes, clangs. You fumble with the lock, click the hasp to. Inside, Sarah Ramsay drums her fists against the door. You follow Doc and walk away. Who will forgive you for this?

Doc slips the key into his vest pocket and you notice his hand is swollen, his fingers puffy and discolored.

"She do that to you?" you ask, and immediately he hides it, mumbles something about catching it in a drawer.

Sarah Ramsay bangs and bangs. In the buckboard, all you hear is the wheels gritting over the road, and you wonder when she'll stop.

A hint of smoke. Doc looks to you to confirm it.

She'll stop when she doesn't hear you anymore, when she gets tired. And what will she do then?

In bed that night, you think of her in the empty house, peeking out at the moon. After the little Norwegian died, you could still hear him pleading for something to eat. It only made you hungrier, and you cursed him. Roll over and hold Marta to you. But again, do you sleep?

Wednesday only one of Chase's women comes to town. Dark, in the simple uniform. You've seen her before, not young but not old, heavy-legged, solid as a Mennonite wife. She takes all morning going store to store, leaving her bundles untended in the wagon. Sugar, coffee, salt. From the chemist, a tin of Paris green, another of London purple. A cask of tar from the hardware, probably to keep flies off the sheep. Ten gallons of kerosene, which she lugs two at a time from Fenton's. Chase is stocking up. Must be telling his people town's corrupt, rife with disease. What can you say—he's right.

You wait till she's trotted off with her load, then go into Fenton's and ask him what she special-ordered for next time.

"Nothing," Fenton says. "Paid in cash as usual." He ducks in back to restock his kerosene. On the counter, the knife display accuses you. You wonder if Fenton knows who chucked the dung under his sidewalk.

Probably.

"What did she buy today?" you ask when he returns, though you already know.

While you're jawing with him, the bell chimes and Mary Condon comes in. She freezes when she sees you, shoots you a vicious look and wheels around, the door ringing behind her. Fenton acts as if he hasn't seen.

But then, when he's finished telling you about the woman from the Colony, and you've done your own shopping, he says, "Heard about Sarah Ramsay."

"Sad thing," you say, and sigh. "Wasn't much else we could do."

"Don't think I could do something like that."

"You do when you have to," you say.

"You'd have to be an awful hard man, I expect."

And though you want to shake him, to scream in his face, you say, "It doesn't do your heart any good, if that's what you mean."

Then back at the jail you're angry with yourself. Why should you apologize to him?

Home, you cook up some bratwurst and drink three ginger beers, then a pint of cider. Leave the dishes undone. Put Amelia to bed with her dolly and open the whiskey, just a nip.

It hits you like a truth, wakes up the blood. You laugh; you want to drink it all. You sing at the kitchen table, tap your feet, slap your knee. "Let's dance," you say, and take Marta in your arms, whirl her through the house like you're nineteen again.

"They all hate me," you say in bed, the liquor swirling the lamplight. You've forgotten Marta's nightshirt.

"They think I don't mind all this."

No they don't, Jacob. You're a good man, everyone knows that.

"Boarding her up like that."

Come, hush now.

"Fenton's right."

Shhh, it's all right. It's all right. Here.

Her arms circle you, and the clean smell of her hair. How pleasingly she fits you, her slim hips to yours, her shoulders, her ribs. Kiss her deeply, run your hands over her cool, perfect skin. Firm and then soft. There, and there. Take her face in your hands. Finally you rise up and make love to her, desperately, after so long, your fingers knitted with hers, your lips to her neck, her ear, confessing how happy she makes you, how, no matter what happens, the two of you will always be together.

"I love you, Marta," you say, surrendering to her, giving up all your sorrow in long, shuddering reaches. "I love you, I love you, I love you."

7

You wait in the dark with your pistol. Heat lightning makes the trees jump, shows you the pale silhouette of the road, the silver glint of the tracks, the dark maw of the canal. You're swapping nights with Bart, trying to keep people on the right side of the line.

The wind has shifted again, and risen, blowing hard from the west. Montello wires Harlow all day; the great gingerbread mansions on the edge of town are burning, their turrets plunging to the ground. Even here, east of Friendship, you can smell the fire coming; the air's heavy and spiced with it. To the west the sky holds a glow, flares like the first minutes after sunset.

You're sure all of town knows. Today Gillett Condon drove his family up to the line and took a whip to Millard when he tried to stop them. Bart has them in the clink over in Shawano, but Millard hurt his eye. He drew his gun, he said, but didn't fire. This is your fault. The doctor there says he might lose it for good.

You wait, pinching mosquitoes from your forehead, slapping at your hair. You've fashioned a blind to one side of the canal, tucked yourself in it like a hunter. It reminds you of guard duty, the river rushing invisible with the spring rains, covering up footsteps, the rustle of branches. At least here there's starlight shining off the leaves, the flash of sheet lightning making everything suddenly present. You watch the road, listen for the scuff of boots, the drumming of hooves.

You've always liked night, the quiet, the bowl of stars above. One August your mother woke you and led you out into the chilly fields to see the stars fall, held your hand and said this was the work of God. She didn't need to; you knew it just by looking up—that all of Creation was a gift from Him, and that you would be a fool not to accept it. How close you felt to everything then, as if you'd found your place at last. You can still do that, simply by tipping your face up, searching between the trees. It's nearly August, you can tell by Orion's belt.

A bullfrog lunks from the canal, and a host of them start up, calling deeply. You shift and rub the back of your neck, a mosquito rolling under your hand. Click the hammer of the Colt back, ease it down again. Stay ready.

Gillett Condon, you think. The little bastard.

Desperate for his family.

Aren't we all?

Not you.

No? You're just mad. Crazy Jacob.

The sky flashes to the east, and the rails are there, running off into the dark, then gone again. Watch the white dust of the road, the sign an oblong shadow in the moonlight. At home Amelia's sleeping, Marta waiting up for you in the rocker. You've got to start eating more, you think. All those bacon and potatoes are playing havoc with your stomach.

A whinny.

No.

You hold your breath. The frogs go on.

Yes, the rattle of metal—a loose stirrup, or a bit clicking on a tooth. Then nothing.

The rattle again, closer.

You scan the road, squint into the dark. The rattle's louder now, almost on top of you, and then you hear the squeak of a saddle—not from the road, but behind you on the towpath.

You wheel and see a blaze on the horse's forehead, floating ghostly. It comes at a walk, the rider trying to be quiet.

Duck your head and push loudly out of the blind, raise your pistol so they'll see it. Step through the brush and onto the towpath, arms over your head.

"I'm warning you to stop," you get out. You'd planned to say more, but the rider cries, "Hyah!" and the horse bolts straight for you.

You level the gun and call, "Halt!" as if this is the war again.

He doesn't. The horse thunders over you, one shoulder catching you smack in the chest. It punches you into the brush, sends your hat and your Colt flying.

You can't breathe. Lie there and gasp a minute, come back to your senses. He caught you just above the heart; already it's tender. You press your thumb into your ribs to see if they're broken. No. Still, you're winded, and it hurts to stand.

Your hat's in a huckleberry bush, not even dusty. Your pistol's gone, and it's dark.

"Bastard!" you say, because you know who it was, should have suspected they'd make a break for it. You're sure, in that moment you could have fired—should have, you think now, scolding yourself—that you saw in the brief noon of the lightning the cowardly face of your friend Fenton.

You crawl on your knees, feeling in the dust for your gun, your chest aching with every heartbeat. It's like a stitch, digging at you. Finally your hand blunders against metal. To your surprise, you find the hammer still cocked. You didn't know you were so close. Holster it, snap the snap. You know it's stupid to fire in anger, and right now you don't trust yourself.

"Should have killed him," you say.

You're quiet. Does that mean you agree?

Bart ought to know, so you climb on the handcar and start off. Every pump of the bar hurts, and you find yourself giving up, coasting through the dark. You hope it's just a charley horse, but when you go to knead the muscle it twinges like a bruise. Your right arm works better, and you try that for a while. Roll past Old Meyer's and the Hermit's lake. The sky lights up, then dies. Finally, the river. You freewheel over the trestle and set the brake, get off and walk along the bank up to Ender's bridge and into town. Everyone's sleeping, it seems.

Knock on Harlow's door. He thumps around, then opens it in his nightshirt, bleary.

"No," he says, "Fenton? You're greening me."

"Saw him with my own two eyes," you assure him, and still he shakes his head. He lifts his key ring off a nail and comes out on the sidewalk in his bare feet and lets you into his office.

"Don't think anyone'll be receiving this time of night," he says, sitting down to the sounder. You say that's all right and thank him, even before he sends your message, then again as he pads off to bed.

You should go back out there but it hurts when you breathe too deeply. The air smells of ash. You're fine, it's just a bruise; you'll be sore tomorrow, that's all.

Why are you always so hopeful? Haven't you learned anything?

The lightning teases you, shows you the road under the oaks, the tidy houses of your neighbors, their kitchen gardens and brick walks. You wonder who's peeking from behind a curtain, how much of town is watching you.

Yesterday you burned down a house with someone in it.

Doc asked you to. It was the Winslets, out west of town. Roland had finally died, and Doc convinced you there wasn't time to bury him, that there was too much to do. While it was true, you still argued with him. But you were so tired, or that's the excuse you make to yourself now. You didn't like it, you said, but you brought the crew out, soaked the baseboards with kerosene, and stood there watching it, angry with everyone but the millhands who'd been pressed into service. You thought of Roland in bed under dirty sheets, and how you'd want to be found. And while you were standing there fuming, you all saw the figure in the attic window, in the invalid room, banging at the glass with her frail bare arms until it fell and shattered on the porch roof. The slow aunt from Eau Claire, you'd all forgotten her. You'd done such a good job there was no chance. She screamed but she was too old to jump, and soon smoke filled the window, the roof collapsed, and the sparks boiled up into the sky. Later, you found her in the basement, light as a husk. When you went to Doc he ducked his head and ran his hands through his hair, and you could see his fingers were puffed with infection. He didn't say he was tired or sick the way you did, didn't make excuses. "She's better off," he said, and before you could light into him, he looked at you so you knew he didn't believe it.

After that, you walked through the empty houses sloshing the jug, calling and calling. Only then did you touch the brand to the love seat, the ottoman, the lampshade. And even though no one in town knows, it's true, they hate you, no matter what Marta says. If they don't, they should. You do.

The door's locked, and you use the moon to find your key. Marta's asleep in the rocker, arms crossed in her lap. You carry her to bed, a sleepy child. It must be all the terrible things that are happening, but she seems more beautiful to you, more precious now that everyone is set against you. She stirs to your touch, moans and coos beneath you, then drops back to sleep after, as if it's all been a dream. For the first time in weeks, you drift off easily, curled around her, your head on her chest.

In the morning you have a black bruise, and Marta badgers you to see Doc. Outside it's cloudy and a light snow is falling, the street covered with a gray dusting of ash.

The Bagwells' wagon stands before their door, bristling with furniture tied on with twine. The whole family's helping, the children with armfuls of clothes.

"Where you headed?" you ask Tom as he knots a sack.

"Shawano," he says, not looking at you.

"They won't let you in."

"We're not staying here," he says. "That's fine for the sick, but there's no reason we should be made to, not with the fire."

"I understand," you say, and you do. You're just not sure what can be done about it. You tell him to be careful and head for Doc's. The street's crosshatched with tracks, a regiment of gray footprints. Must be an inch of the stuff. You try not to run.

The ash sits on the hitching rail, dirties the trough water. His door's locked but there's no sign saying he's out making calls. You thump and thump, and finally he appears at the curtain, just his head sticking out. He waves and disappears again, then comes back a minute later in a dressing gown and lets you in, stands there staring at the fall of ash like a child.

His face is lined from his pillow, and his hand is bandaged. At one corner of his mouth is a black crust of blood. When he tells you to have a seat, his voice is hoarse, barely a squeak, as if his throat's closing.

You stare, unable to say a word.

He looks disappointed in you—or in himself? The two of you face each other like a gunfight.

"Hell," he croaks, "guess there's no point hiding it now."

"When did you know?" you ask, thinking it's not possible. He made it so long you thought he was like you, that he couldn't get it. For a minute you wish you could. Now you're going to be alone.

"Couple days ago. Not long."

You look at the carpet as if it holds some clue. He's apologizing, but you shrug it off. "You tell Irma yet?"

"Not yet."

"Better wire her. No telling how long you'll be able to. I mean, with the fire."

"I know what you mean."

You say you're sorry and he just nods, shifts his paperweight with his good hand. Goddamn him.

"Sorry I'm running out on you," he says, and tries to smile. He's hard to hear, and you lean forward, toward the desk.

"Any idea what you're going to do?" he asks.

"Take the healthy ones out on the freight." You say it like

it's been in you all along. It has, you just don't think it'll work.

"Keep them in it," he says. "Bring 'em right back after."

"I'll have Bart to help keep 'em in line."

He nods, watching the ashes fall. "That's good. That's what I was going to suggest."

You nod back a thanks, let him know you appreciate his trust in you. "I'll start west of town and move east."

"Don't worry about the sick ones. There's nothing you can do."

"I know."

"Chase gives you any trouble, you just leave him be."

"I will."

"Don't waste your time on him."

"I won't," you say, but rightly he doesn't believe you.

"Jacob," he says, and coughs, makes you wait. "You can't save all of them. That's not your job here."

You grimace to show you register it. Why can't you just agree with him?

"I tell you about Fenton?" you say, and tell him.

"The son of a bitch," he says.

He comes over and peels your shirt back to take a look at it. You can smell his hand, the blood on his breath. "Yep, that's some bruise." He presses it with his thumbs so you groan. "Nothing broken though."

You'll have to get Harlow to send a message to Montello, ask the railroad to hold the freight where it crosses the river south of town. Wire Bart to fill him in. Harlow can spread the word here while you round up everyone to the west. The freight comes through around three so you've still got a full six hours. You know it won't be enough. You won't get everyone.

You stop in the middle of your explanation.

"What?" Doc asks.

"Someone ought to be ringing the bell."

"Cyril."

"You hear him this morning?" you ask, because you didn't.

He shakes his head, and you think of Cyril squeezing your hand after services, complimenting your sermon, then moving on as if there were people behind him.

"I'll have to get someone," you say.

"See if John Cole's got a man to spare."

"Good idea." You get up and fit your hat on, then stop.

"Go on," Doc says.

"I'll come back and look in on you."

"There's nothing you can do for me," he says.

"I'll look in and let you know what Chase is up to."

"I'll be here," he says, unconcerned, but then he stands and offers you his hand. The two of you shake as if sealing a pact.

"Take care of Marta and Amelia," he calls after you, and you promise you will.

Outside, Carl Soderholm rattles past in his buggy, his bay mare raising a gray cloud. He sees you but doesn't wave, doesn't slow, just heads east out of town toward Ender's bridge. As you cross the street, the air bites at your eyes, coats your tongue. Fenton's door is open. Look inside, and the place is topsy-turvy, the shelves empty, the floor littered with yard goods. It reminds you of Kentucky, the looting. Wade through the clutter. His gun rack is empty, the lock sawed off. The entire display of knives is missing.

Harlow pokes his head in with a telegram. "Bart's got trouble out on the line."

You're knee-deep in smashed sacks of flour and ask him to read it to you.

"Says a deputy of his had to shoot someone."

"Who?"

"Emmett Nelligan. Just winged him, it says. Got the whole family in the pokey."

High-step over the mess, read the wire yourself. Bart's raised a barricade so no one else tries to break through. There's still no word on Millard. You swear and tell Harlow what to wire him back. You tell him the whole plan and what he needs to do.

"Montello's still sending," Harlow says.

"I don't care," you say. "They're fools if they stay there. After the freight gets in, tell them to get on it. And get someone to ring that bell."

West of town the sky is darker, and the wind has picked up, the hot ash stinging your cheeks. It's slippery, and you can't ride as fast as you like. Your chest doesn't hurt as much, just the remnants of a bruise. Someone's finally ringing the bell, a slow, steady toll. Past the wreckage of Millie and Elsa's, Winslet's, Heilemann's. It looks like Kentucky during the war, those endless hollows you marched through, the carcasses of hogs bloating in the sun, children hiding behind their mothers. Past Ramsay's still boarded up. You're tempted to stop at their gate, run up to the porch to see if she's alive. Probably not; it's been days. On the way back, you promise, if you have time. The horizon's black as a tornado. When you pass the field full of Terfel's sheep, you can't even smell them.

You race all the way to the gap at Cobb's tunnel, where John Cole and his crew are widening the fire line. The air is filled with cinders; they patter like sleet in the trees. The grass catches fire, and the men frantically stamp on it, dance in a huddle as if it's a rattler, then pick up their shovels again. While you're talking with John, a doe zigzags through the crew and bounds past you, headed for town.

"Don't stay too long now," you warn John.

"Don't you worry about that," he says. "You just make sure that train's there."

Back past the *Q* for the swamper camp, posted by a corduroy road running back into the pines. There's no one there, you reason, and if they're dead, you can't fire the place because it's in the middle of the woods. It's that simple. So why are you stopped by the sign? Why stand there debating it, wondering how your bike will stand up to the ruts?

It's been a week.

Don't waste your time, Doc said.

He meant Chase.

He meant the dead.

There, that's where you disagree with him. The dead need to be taken care of. Isn't that your duty?

It's just one of your jobs, and right now it's a luxury. The air's stinging with cinders. Be sensible. Get on your bike and ride.

Past Dole's and Schnackmeier's and Margaret Kyne's. You leave them to die by fire.

Maybe they're already dead.

You hope so. You picture them on the floor of the pantry, laid out in the front hall. Probably at the door, their last effort spent rattling the lock, cursing your name.

What, do you want to say you're sorry? What good does that do? You killed them sure as the disease. Have you saved *any* of them?

Not Amelia. Not Marta. Not Doc.

The first house you stop at is Paulsen's. The windows are shuttered. You rap at the door. A rumble, then footsteps, the jingle of a key, and Henrik Paulsen opens the door holding a shotgun from the hip.

"Stand back, if you would," he says, and you do. "You ain't sick, are you?"

"No," you say, and ask the same of him.

"No. Ain't planning on it neither."

You keep your hands in front of you and explain the freight, and still he doesn't budge. He comes out on the porch, looking around for your deputies, then forces you down the steps and into the yard. "I ain't about to get mixed up with any town folk if I can help it."

"Look over yonder," you say, and slowly point to the massed blackness.

"John Cole still working that line of his?" he asks.

"Yep."

"Then no telling where it'll go. Ain't that right?"

Agree with him, start in again with the plan.

"Where's everyone else?" he asks, waving the barrel around. "If you're taking everyone, where are they?"

You can't answer him.

"No sir," he says, "we made it this far, we'll take our chances. If worse comes to worst, we can always go down the well."

You'd forgotten about that. It's an old Indian trick, though with the size of this fire, you don't give it much chance of working. You tell Henrik that, admitting, though, that it's possible, that your plan's not foolproof either.

"To each his own," he says, and when you nod at this logic, he lowers the gun. "No hard feelings, Sheriff."

"None," you say, and drop your hands. "I'll look in on you after."

"I'd be obliged."

Riding away, you're not surprised. People don't like to leave their homes. They'll bundle up the silver and bury it in the front yard, dig it up warm after the fire moves through. Let the stock run free, fend for themselves. You understand better than anyone, people don't like to give up what they're used to.

Yancey Thigpen's already made a break for it. His horses are wandering the back pasture, harnessless, sneezing and waving their heads at the ashes. He's locked the barn so they won't rush back in, left his own front door open. You're glad he's gone, just hope he's not out at the line.

Fred Lembeck says he'll get his things together, calmly,

as if he hadn't planned to leave. For some reason it makes you angry. You'd think a man with one arm would get used to thinking ahead.

"Just take what you need," you say, then think how ridiculous it sounds. Tomorrow there may be nothing left of the house. Take everything, you think.

"I'll be more than a minute," he calls from the back.

"We'll meet at the river," you tell him, "right below Ender's bridge," and when you're sure he's heard you, move on.

At Huebner's you're surprised to find Carl there with his family.

"I thought you were in Shawano," you say.

"I was, but I couldn't stay there. Not with this."

"I suppose I understand," you say, and go over the plan. You're getting faster at it, and the more you explain it, the better it seems. You leave Terfel's convinced it'll work.

The next place is Ramsay's, and against your better judgment you slow and then hop off at the gate. It's latched, the post capped with ash, the sign still warning people away. Parts of the Q have chipped and fallen to the floor, but the lock's solid. You hammer at the door, then listen.

Nothing. But you expected that.

Wander across the porch and peek through the boards. It's dim inside. Broken dishes, what might be blood on the rug. You call her name, wait.

Walk around back, then the other side. The boards are intact, and you climb the porch steps again and pull out the key.

Fast around the downstairs, then up. You smell her first. She's in a doorway, her legs fallen awkwardly across the hall, the rest of her in the bedroom. Flies lift from a pile of dried vomit. It's yellow, dotted with tiny red specks—matchheads.

How cruel you've become, thinking it's better than Paris green. Then it's true, you've gone absolutely mad, utterly indifferent to those you know. Every day there's less of you. How you'd love to stop, to follow her. Your stomach clenching around the chemicals would be a penance, an offering before the release. But who would take care of Friendship then?

You kneel and carefully recite a prayer. Eyes shut tight, you picture Sarah Ramsay in the kitchen, cutting the heads off matches two by two, building a little pile. Gather breath and ask Him for strength, for forgiveness, then stand and walk away, leave her sinfully unattended.

The road is trackless again, a pond of ash. From town, the bell sounds muffled and dull. The wind is hot and hard, pushing you along; it lifts your hat, bites at the back of your neck. Every flake makes you grunt. You can see why hell is filled with fire. Lord knows how John Cole and his crew are doing.

Just outside of town a swallow drops from the sky, plummets into the sere cornfield beside you. You turn in time to see a whole flock falling, bending the dead stalks, thumping into the dust like hail, a rain of stones. They come down around you, their soft bodies pelting your back. They cover the road, dead yet perfect. When you bend to touch one, its feathers are hot, its eye boiled white.

You check the sky—empty again, and then a crow wings slowly over the woods, untouched.

Is this prophecy? But you can make nothing of it. There's no sin Friendship needs to redress. There's no reason behind any of this.

You stop in at home and get Marta out of bed and dressed, set her on the love seat with Amelia. Tell them the plan as you get them ready.

You'll be back, she asks, and you reassure her. She understands you have to help the others first, she doesn't question it. You kiss her to show how grateful you are for her. She knows.

Just don't leave us here, she jokes.

"I won't," you say, and wave, then lock the door behind you.

Harlow's waiting for you outside the jail, a wire in his hand. The bell's deafening. "Montello's down," he shouts, and waves the paper tape to prove it.

It's their last message.

FIRE HERE. MUST LEAVE SOONEST. ADVISE SAME.

"When'd this come in?"

Harlow counts the perforations on the tape. "'Leven-forty. Bout ten minutes ago."

You reach for your watch, sure it's earlier.

No. Where did the time go?

"Shawano still up?" you ask him.

"Already sent it. Haven't heard back yet. I'm sure Bart's busy. Lots of folks been headed that way."

"He can take care of them," you shout, mostly to convince yourself. "Who's ringing the bell?"

"Cyril."

"Where was he this morning?"

"I don't know," he says, and shrugs when you press him. "Maybe he slept late."

Across the street, the crew from the mill is tossing buckets of water on Fenton's roof. Let it burn, you want to say. None of it makes any sense.

Just as you're going inside to get your rifle, John Cole and his crew hightail it in, swerving, their team foaming black around the mouth. They all jump off and rush around to haul someone off the bed. You run out and see one of the men is missing his eyebrows, his face a mask of soot. They're carrying a heavy man on a makeshift litter; he's burnt black as a minstrel show, his clothes stuck to his skin.

"Fire jumped the line," John says, steering him toward Doc's office.

"You can't go in there," you say. "He's got the sickness. Put him in here." You throw open the door to the jail and they lay him on the floor.

He coughs, moans without moving his lips. It's Kip Cheyney, you didn't even recognize him. His fingers show through the holes in his gloves—bubbles and bloody patches.

"I'll see what Doc says," you promise, and leave them standing around like mourners.

Bang the glass, the frame. Call.

You wait, expecting him to part the curtain, his breath a whistle. You hope he's changed out of the dressing gown.

Rattle the knob, call again.

John comes out on the sidewalk. "Isn't he there?"

You borrow a glove and punch the window in. John wants to follow you through the parlor, but you turn him back, remind him Doc's sick.

He's in the last room, laid out on top of the covers, still in the gown. His eyes are closed, his lips open. One arm hangs off the side, the back of his hand touching the floor. On the nightstand sits an empty vial of laudanum, and propped against the lamp, a letter in rich stationery for Irma.

"Goddamn it," you say. "Goddamn it all."

You squat and raise Doc's arm, lay it beside him, quickly offer the same prayer you gave Sarah Ramsay. Doc. Goddamn. You feel like something needs to be said in his behalf but it's like a sermon you don't know how to start. What does it mean to say he was a good man? But he was. He helped others, he loved Irma. It *does* count for something.

Rise and slip the letter in your jacket. Go to the cabinet. There must be a salve for burns here somewhere. Carl Soderholm would know, but he's gone like the rest of them, the cowards, and you rifle through the jars and boxes and tubes, interrogating labels.

Doc lies there. You're not disappointed in him, you're not, but you drop a bottle and can't stop yourself from kicking the broken pieces and shouting out a curse. There's no time. Goddamn it all is right.

You open one that looks like earwax and smells like bag

balm. You figure Kip would be better off asleep and find a vial of valerian drops.

"Just follow the instructions on it," you tell John. "And don't say anything around town about Doc being sick."

He nods, promises.

Tell him you're headed out to the Colony, that you'll be back to take the others down the river. You want John to have them ready when you get back, everyone who's coming. They can bring Kip in the wagon.

He looks at you, confused.

"Talk to Harlow," you say. "He knows the plan."

You grab your rifle and head for Ender's bridge. The road is mobbed with tracks, and in the ashes lies a flattened bird-cage, a canary still in it, clinging sideways to its perch. You pick the twisted thing up and the bird flutters and beats its wings. Pry the bars wide with your knife and set it free, toss the cage aside.

Don't congratulate yourself. Think of Doc, letting him rot there like an animal.

Why can't you understand him? Sarah Ramsay. Millie.

Because it's a temptation you've almost fallen into.

Because it's wrong.

The handcar's where you left it. You lay your rifle on the floor and pump, the bruise reminding you of last night. You understand Fenton. During the siege, men would run out from behind the horses and be shot dead rather than lie there another night. How many things in life come down to patience, the willingness to accept, to wait for a better chance.

The woods rush up and swallow you, and the bell retreats

into the distance. Cyril missing daybreak. It's getting so you can't depend on anyone.

Not Doc, you don't mean that.

He did the best he could.

Did he?

You concentrate on the bar, don't try to answer for him. Your shoulders hurt, and your collarbone's sore. Lean into the curve and onto the Nokes spur, the tracks rusty with disuse, ferns thrashing the front of the car. The sky's taken on a jaundiced tinge, like before a storm. You wonder if Chase has led them down into the mines, then wish you'd thought of it before. Too late now, you'd never get everyone out here in time. Maybe he's filled the mansion with the sick; they must be overflowing, the nurses careworn, harried. You imagine that he's burned the great house to the ground, sent it shuddering earthward like Montello's, the nurses still in it. Revelations, the Last Times, the fire that burns the earth clean. He set it with the kerosene the stout woman bought the other day. It should have been obvious. What kind of a penny-dreadful detective are you?

No, you would have seen it, even in this muck. And Chase is like you, isn't that what you tried to tell Doc? He'll send his healthy down south of town, after the circus, keep the sick ones here and tend to them. He's responsible to his flock, something you doubt in yourself now.

But there's a chance the schoolboy rumors are true, and after everything you've seen this week, you wouldn't rule out a terrible ceremony, a communion with each believer lining up to kiss the diseased lips of their Messiah.

Anything is possible out here. The trees seem to confirm this, the woods full of shadows, fire raining from the sky. It's a relief to turn the last curve of the spur and see the mansion still standing, the barns and corncribs and rock-walled slurry. And then you see there's no one there, not a single chicken.

Pull the brake lever, get your rifle and hop off. Wind in the trees, the patter of ashes. The gate is an arch of raw branches, the Holy Light sign swinging beneath it. REV. S. P. CHASE, it says. You cross a long swath of yard toward the mansion. No footprints, hoofprints, nothing. The windows are shuttered, the porch stairs caked with ash.

Beyond the mansion stands the carriage house, also closed, then a row of cottages with saints' names above the doors. Sebastian, Stephen, Thomas. All martyrs. None of them are locked. Inside they have identical furniture—a single bed, a desk, a simple chair—and each is tidy, un-lived in.

The formal gardens are planted with vegetables, the grand fountain in the middle used to water them. Despite the drought, their beans are high climbers, their tomatoes fat as apples. All of it's dusted with ash, a slick skin on the water.

The mines, you think.

He's smarter than you, he's taken better care of his people.

Yes, but it was easier—they listen to him.

Turn, the rifle loose in one hand, pointed toward the ground. The chapel, another barn, the chicken house with its rows of windows. You slog across the yard, leaving tracks, and as you angle for the chapel you hear—lightly, as if far off—singing.

It grows as you come closer, blinking away flakes. The stairs bear faint traces of footprints, the stoop the twin arcs of the doors. You lean your ear to the crack.

They're in there, singing.

You take advantage of the noise to lean the rifle against the stair railing, then open the door.

It's a small congregation is your first thought, the seats half-filled, maybe twenty of them. And then you notice the cots along the walls, the sick lying there while the rest of them bellow *Jesus Our Redeemer*. You know it well; only your disbelief prevents you from joining in.

Chase is up front in plain white robes, bearish beside the pulpit, the stout woman at his right hand. He tips his chin at you, leads the singing in a fatherly, half-spoken baritone, keeping his place with a finger. Some of the members sit, some stand; some of the ones on cots are asleep, others tended by nurses.

The song ends, and with a rumble everyone sits down. A long hard coughing as Chase mounts the pulpit. He pauses and looks up again, smiling, as if he has good news.

"Deacon Hansen," he booms, and raises a hand, as if blessing you.

Faces turn, and you give them a nod, a tight grimace of a smile.

"You have something for us?" Chase asks.

"The fire's coming," you say, so they can all hear.

"We know," he says.

"I'm taking a train of everyone who's not sick out of town."

"Everyone who *isn't* sick."

"That's right."

"How about those who are?"

"There's nothing can be done for them. I'm sorry."

"Thank you, Deacon," Chase says. "We all appreciate your offer, but I'm afraid it's come too late for us to accept."

"There's time," you say, and start to go on about the train, three o'clock, how many people can fit in a boxcar.

"It's not that," he says calmly, "I wish it were that simple. I'm afraid all of us—" And here he spreads his hands to include everyone in the room, the remnants of his entire flock. "I'm afraid we're all similarly afflicted."

You hadn't expected this, and so you don't have an answer.

You can hear the ash settling on the roof above. "What are you going to do?"

"Right now," he says, "we're going to pray."

And you know why you bow your head along with the rest of them, why you recite the lines. They're going to stay and die together, pay the price for what they believe in, willingly, and this, this you completely understand.

8

The fire doesn't come in a line, a front of troops sweeping through. It foots through the dry woods like a spy, rides the burning wind. As you pump for town, the sky whirls, thick and dark as a twister, shedding debris. Smoldering pinecones rain down like incendiaries, starting spot fires in the brush. The trees thrash, toss off their leaves; dust devils kick up along the tracks, then vanish. You have your bandanna tied over your nose, and still each breath is like working in a furnace. It's all taking too long, but you don't dare free a hand to read your watch. Any other day you could hear the freight puffing south of town, the clean scream of its whistle, but the wind is deafening, the trees, and you pump, trusting you'll beat it to the main line.

Where the spur switches in, the tracks are covered with ash, but it's falling so hard that you can't be sure. In the distance, a steam whistle calls a long note, and you turn, expecting to see the huge engine bearing down on you, the driver highballing it, the brakeman unable to stop. Nothing but a blizzard of ash—and then it calls again, and you look north, toward town. It's the mill, signaling the fire's slow approach. It calls and calls, a child that won't stop crying.

Who's doing it? you wonder.

Not Cyril. John Cole probably.

Bend and drive the bar down, then back up hard. Your chest has gone beyond a knot, the muscle like a knife. The whistle's a good sign, you think; the mill's still standing. And John Cole's got sense enough to get out of there while he can. You hope it's not Cyril.

All of this is your fault.

A hail of branches flails you, an acorn ricocheting off the bar, and you pump harder. In the woods to your right a small fire jumps in the dimness, lurks there like an animal. The river's not far now, just another curve and then the long, slow grade running up to the bridge. You hope Harlow has them ready. If it's not three yet, it's darn close.

Turn the curve and they're ahead, standing on the track—only a few of them, maybe seven, all lugging carpetbags and in bandannas, a clutch of robbers. Harlow, Cyril, some of John's crew. Not a woman among them. Kip Cheyney's laid out on a cart, a leather apron draped over him to keep the embers off. You throw the brake on too hard, and it pitches you against the bar, another bruise. Fred Lembeck comes running up, his one arm out for balance.

"Is she coming?" he asks. In the roar, it's hard to hear.

"Should be," you shout, and mark the time—five minutes till. "Where is everybody?"

"The river, most of 'em," he says, and points, and you crane to see what's left of Friendship, thirty people milling waist-deep in the filthy water, tossing hatfuls of it on each other. Some you haven't seen since the beginning of all this—Karmanns, Armbrusters. Their possessions litter the near bank: clocks, pots, a sewing machine wrapped in a quilt. The children are swaddled in sopping blankets, their mothers slapping at their hair. Crying, keening. Katie Merrill holds a lacy parasol; the cinders hit it, smolder a minute, then burn through. A lone cow wanders among them, lowing, shouldering people aside, and atop the water floats a host of fish killed by the heat.

"Lot of folks couldn't wait," Fred says. "Didn't think the train would make it."

You know who those folks are. Emmett Nelligan. Bagwells. And why should they believe in you, Crazy Jacob the Undertaker?

You look down the track. The sky to the west is a dark wall.

"It'll make it," you say. And you do believe it. At this point, what choice do you have?

Kip Cheyney's passed out, probably from the valerian. You pat Cyril on the shoulder, glad to see him, his sleeping in forgiven. Harlow gives you a nod of confidence.

Palm your watch again. It's foolish; do you really think they're following their schedule today?

You part John's crew and stand in the middle of the bridge. What's left of Friendship looks up at you, waits for your word, and you think of Chase, how you have even less to give them.

Or maybe it's the same—a prayer.

It's not enough for them, admit it. They want to be saved while they're still in this world. Like you, no?

"All right," you holler. "I want everyone up on the tracks right now. Leave your things, you won't need them."

You have to tell them again, then go down to help them out, trusting Fred to watch the tracks. They splash across the flats and crawl up the bank, slippery with ash. They squish with each step, their clothes clinging to them, a sec-ond skin the color of mud. Cyril almost falls in. You're parched from the handcar, and dip a hand in the river; it's gray and tastes of lye, and you spit it out.

"Sheriff!" Fred calls from the bridge. He's pointing fran-tically down the track, and you don't have to hear the rest of what he says.

Scrabble up the bank and sprint for the bridge. Even in this light, you can see the lush plume of the freight loom-ing above the curve.

You shove the handcar onto the siding and grab your rifle. Get everyone ready, the men a skirmish line four deep on the tracks, with you at the head of them. The plume seems to grow blacker the closer it gets, a rich charcoal, and still you can't hear the steam, only the trees tilting in the wind. You step forward and raise the sight to your eye, try to guess where the engine will clear the pines.

This must be what it feels like holding up a train.

Well, that's what you're doing, isn't it?

The face of the train turns the curve—cowcatcher, head-lamp, stack. You're high, and bring the sight down, the post steady on the engine. You don't see the driver, and think of popping off a shot, just a warning. You can hear the chuff of the boiler now, feel the railbed give under the train's weight, the gravel ballast crunching underfoot.

You fire a shot high above the cab, the crack lingering, singing in your ear like an insect.

Another, the same place.

The driver pokes his nose out the window and blows the whistle. You wave the rifle, then sight in on him. He ducks and tugs the whistle again.

It's not a hard decision. If he doesn't stop, you'll kill him for the sake of these people. You've made up your mind, justified it.

How easy it seems, this commandment, but just look at you.

No one behind you moves, not a man jack of them. You suddenly love them for this. You know you can do it.

The rails sing, and you stay on the window, getting your breathing ready.

His glove comes up, you tense, and then the steel shrieks as he lays on the brakes. The driving wheels skid along the rails, a piercing squeal like taking a grindstone to a huge knife. You want to cover your ears, and then it's bearable again. The grade slows the train, holds the great mass back.

And still you don't lower the gun, leave it on him to let him know you're in charge. This has nothing to do with them, or anyone, just the two of you. You know that's not true, but when you finally drop the barrel, you nearly feel cheated. He would have run you through. And you were ready, there's no denying it.

He's your age, with a boiled face and a fringe of whiskers, and he's angry as a drunk Canuck. He scowls down from his perch as if he's the one holding the gun. You make a show of putting it away.

"Just what the hell is all this?"

"Be obliged if you could ride us to Shawano," you say.

"Sign back at the tunnel says I'm not sposed to take on riders."

"*I* posted that sign."

"So now I'm sposed to take these people on your say-so, is that it?"

"None of them are sick, I can vouch for them. They can all fit in a boxcar, you don't even have to look at them. Whole thing won't take five minutes. Otherwise it's the fire."

He looks back at the sky, the smoking twigs and leaves dropping all around the tender. He regards you, the rifle down by your side, finger still on the trigger.

"Three minutes," he says. "And I ain't gettin' anywhere near 'em."

There's a panic at first, a lot of clawing at the door to get it open. You have to holler at them to let Kip Cheyney through, but they do. The car actually has a load of tractor parts from Montello. The women sit on top of the crates, the men lean their muddy backs against them. It's windowless, so you leave the door open to give them some air.

"That everyone?" you ask, and when no one answers, you run to the middle of the bridge and call down at the water. The cow's headed for Ender's. Just as you're fumbling to hook the handcar on, John Cole comes racing down the bank. The boiler's building up steam, hissing like a teakettle, water dripping from the piston. You put a hand up for the brakeman to wait, then wave John on.

"Where's Marta?" he asks, breathless.

"I've still got to go back," you say, which is the truth, and point to the handcar.

"Better hurry. The roof of the mill just caught."

"Get in," you tell him, then run up front and climb into the cab with the driver.

"I can tend her myself, thank you," he says, then when you don't budge, yanks the cord above his head and deafens you, tips a lever, and the train lurches forward.

You know every pebble of this stretch, every tree. The freight seems slower than your handcar, takes forever to get up steam. The engine hesitates and the couplings clatter, the cars knock, then pull taut again. The driver doesn't look at you, just peeks at the rifle, as if he might wrestle you for it. You're still ready to shoot him, though you find your mind wandering, resting a second, going over what you have to do. There's no time, but you promised Marta. There's probably not time to take care of them *and* Doc proper. And then you skirt the far edge of the Hermit's lake—the water black between the trees—and you remember him.

He'll know enough to jump in the water, you've already talked to him about that. Crazy maybe, but he's no fool.

Like you?

The marsh is dried up on both sides, and in the cattail flats you can see a smattering of fires. The ash is just as thick here, and when you lean out to look behind, it seems the fire's pursuing you, the sky violent and backlit, shimmering like some artist's vision of Hell. For no reason, you check your watch; the time doesn't even register. You wonder if Shawano is far enough, or if it might be best to just keep going east, run the tender empty.

"I ain't stopping for no one till *I* think it's safe," the driver seconds.

You thank him for taking Friendship on.

"Not like I had much say in it," he says.

He's got the throttle opened up, and you bump along, the trucks clicking. Almost there. You wonder how Henrik Paulsen is doing with his family. You think you should have found a way to convince him, move him with a sermon. Too late now.

Too late for a lot of them. How many did you leave?

Chase. The entire Colony.

You should have had a plan, you and Doc.

The canal slides alongside you, the towpath busy with hoofprints. You think of Fenton; that was just last night. Two weeks ago you loved the heat, the lull of summer. It's astonishing how quickly things fall apart.

Directly ahead, a column of smoke lifts from the woods, and the driver slows, leans forward, squinting. The smoke rolls straight up, a black pillar, and you're afraid it's another train.

"What is it?" you ask.

"It's on the tracks." He points, and, in the distance, as you thunder for it, you can see a heap of burning ties. It's right at the town line.

Old Bart. Just like Kentucky.

"Don't slow down," you order him.

"We can't run through it."

"I'm telling you to."

"We'll hang her up," he shouts, and keeps his eyes on you so you know. You wish you'd closed the door, then you could just crouch down.

"All right," you say.

The driver inches back the throttle and you ease up to the ties, scanning the woods for an ambush. They're stacked in a neat tepee, like a campfire. Bart must have just lit them; you can still smell the kerosene.

It's him, with Millard, a patch over his eye. They sidle out of your blind, hatless. You keep the rifle beneath the lip of the window, give them a wave. They look down the length of the train, then back up at you.

"What all you got here, Jake?" Bart asks, and you wonder if it was Fenton who told him. The son of a bitch, it must have been.

"Everyone that's left. We had to leave the sick ones behind."

"Quarantine all done with then?"

"Yep," you say.

"I thought Doc said another week."

"I can vouch for everyone here. We won't even leave the train, we'll just—"

"You know I can't let you," he says, and his face changes, turns stern. "I been seeing your people all day."

"Kip Cheyney's got some burns need attention."

"I'm sorry, Jake."

"None of these people are sick," you protest.

"I can't risk it."

"What did you do with the rest of them—Emmett Nelligan and them?"

"All I could do—turned 'em around."

"Where are they all?"

"That's not my lookout, or yours."

Bart starts and draws on John Cole, who's come out of the boxcar.

"Get back in there," Bart warns him, then yells it when John asks what's happening.

"You can't do this," John says. He's a big man, and Bart has to step back. "I'll tell you right now, we're not going back after all this."

"You shut up," Bart says, "and you get back in there."

John still won't go, starts to holler, threatening him. "Goddamn you, we're not going back!"

"Get back in there before I shoot you!"

Millard reaches for his pistol, and you find you've got your rifle on Bart, who's got his Colt aimed at John's face.

You see where it's leading, and what's left to you. There are thirty-some people in that car. The fire's not going to stop.

"Bart," you call, "leave him."

"Get back in there!"

John turns to appeal to you. He wants to rush him, take the gun, shove it in his face.

"Get back in there," you say, and now Bart sees the rifle.

"You better just drop that right now," he says, and turns the pistol on you.

"I'm warning you," you say. "So help me, I'll put a buttonhole through you."

"I can't let these people into my town, you know that."

"I don't have time for this." And you don't. He isn't going to listen to you. It's simple when you get down to it. You've been hopeful for too long. Look what it's gotten you. Doc, Marta, everyone you love.

"Jake, understand now—"

"Will you let us through?"

"I can't."

"You won't."

"Can't," he says, and stands firm. You know him, you know it's true.

"I gave you fair warning," you say. And can you say what moves you—is it like Chase and his people, the Hermit and his ducks? Is it some kind of love? Because you shoot him through the heart, turn and drop Millard where he stands.

"Jesus God," the driver says behind you.

"Get those off there," you call to John.

He doesn't move, stands there entranced. Say it again, then jump down and start hauling them off with the gaff on the catcher. In a minute, the rest of the mill crew pitches in. You let them finish it, turn away from the flames and look at Bart and Millard, faceup in the dust. John joins you, but you don't say anything to him. You walk back to the hand-car and start uncoupling it. The chains are hot, and you have to tug your gloves on.

You're sorry and you're not. You're sorry for Millard; he didn't know any better. Bart you're still angry with. Of all people, he should know what Friendship means to you. None of these people are sick, but he'd never believe you. You would have sat there and died like Chase's people, when there's no need.

Does this excuse you?

No.

Is this evil?

You're not sure.

Then what is it?

You don't know.

You unhook the handcar, give it a push with your foot. The bar seesaws, then stops, waits for you to climb on.

Walk up front, past Bart and Millard, still lying there draining. The faces in the boxcar follow you, but you don't acknowledge them. It seems plain that while you love these people you don't belong with them, that even in caring for them you've managed to damn yourself.

Give John the rifle, tell him to ride with the driver. The

others hop back in the car, arrange themselves on the crates. You leave them, head the other direction. No one protests; they know what you've done.

"You be careful, Sheriff," Harlow calls.

"You too," you say.

Cyril waves, and for a minute you wish you could go with them, explain. But that passes.

On the handcar, you look back. Bart and Millard are still there, the plume's pouring up from the boiler. You wait till they move out before you pump for town. To the west, the sky is like night, a red glow just above the horizon.

Your chest is sore from doing nothing, but the grade helps you. The canal is an ashpit, no hint of water. You keep looking back; the train doesn't seem to move, and then you turn a curve and it's gone and the marsh is on fire, the cattails waving like flaming brands. The Hermit's lake flits in the trees, slips back.

Ridiculous, but you're worried about him. You've always included him as part of Friendship; that hasn't changed.

And what about the sick, can you dismiss them so easily? What about Bart and Millard? Where do your responsibilities stop?

Sometimes you have to choose.

But don't you see the vanity in your decisions? Aren't you at all sorry? Why do you need to believe you're right? In the end, do you think that will save you?

No.

The fire's louder toward town, the constant rush of a waterfall. The bridge is intact, and Ender's, just up the river.

The bank's littered with their possessions. The cow's gone, only the fish floating. You run for town, wishing you had your bicycle, every breath hurting your throat. The wind blows so hard you have to lean into it, and the dust peppers your skin.

The mill's already gone, the hose of the water engine burned through. The lumberyard is a field of black ash, a smudge. You pause to take it in, then think better of it when a maddened horse crashes past, dragging a buggy on its side, one wheel busted to the hub. You know it—it's Soderholm's bay mare—and you wonder what Bart did with them.

Turned them back, he said.

Which was his right. Why are you still trying to justify it?

Friendship is still standing. The bell tower's untouched, you mark it from a distance, and when you reach Main Street you see everything's fine: the empty *County Record* office, the bank, the foundry. Fenton's, Doc's, the jail, the livery, Ritter's. All standing abandoned, doors flung open, windows smashed, goods strewn over the whole street.

Who would do this? you think, but the proof is irrefutable—someone did. There's Doc's blotter, and your Wanted posters thrown around like a joke. For a minute you forget what you're doing and stand there disbelieving, in a rage, crushed by what they've done to your town.

The air is filled with cinders. An ember lights the sidewalk on fire and you stomp it with your boots.

Across the street, a branch lands on Fenton's roof, and the shingles flash and catch. You run to the trough but it's empty. Throw the bucket away and race for home, your eyes stinging.

Under the oaks there's just a dusting of ash. No one's gone through your neighbors'; their shutters are battened tight against the fire, their owners hopeful. You expect your house to be gutted—hope against hope—but it's fine, and you're grateful. You vault the fence and dig for your keys, sure of your purpose. At least this promise you can keep.

Marta's on the love seat, holding Amelia. Her head's bent, as if leaning down to rub noses with her.

You sit beside her, tip her chin up and give her a kiss.

She looks at you, her eyes milky, her mouth fixed in a grimace, lips pulled back from her perfect teeth. You should have used more fluid. You almost want to say you're sorry.

You are.

"It's time," you say.

But I don't want to go.

You don't want to argue, and kiss her again, hold her to you a last time. She understands.

Fetch Amelia's coffin from the root cellar and lay her in it again, bless her.

The backyard's covered with ash, the garden neatly outlined. You dig in the same spot under the crab apple, take the cross from above the crib, but this time it seems you say the words with less feeling, rush, hurrying to get it done. It's wrong, and back inside it nags at you.

You're sorry you don't have a box for Marta. What a waste, all that planed cedar downstairs in the jail. You would have made a lovely one, taken pains with it, maybe a window for her face, silver fittings. Something worthy of her.

Pry the cross off the wall above your bed.

The plot's not deep enough either.

"I'm trying," you say, and the ash falls hot on the back of your neck.

She's soft in your arms, and her perfume's strong. You carry her through the hallway, her feet nudging the wall.

Lay her beside Amelia, fix her hair with your fingers. Her blue dress, she'd be happy with that.

"I did the best I could," you say.

I know, Jacob.

You tell her you love her, turn the first shovel of earth. The wind lifts the dust, scatters it like ash. You do it almost purposely slow. Are you hoping the fire might light here and consume you? Or is it reverence, a debt you know you owe her?

Please don't leave me.

"No, I have to."

Eyes closed, you recite a prayer for the dead from memory, then linger there, unsure of what to do. It's that time in the ceremony when you go over to the bereaved and lead them from the churchyard, the rest of their friends a slow procession. Today there's no wake. You're alive; it seems another failure. How many times can you say you're sorry? Is it true, after all you've preached, that you'd rather live a sinner than surrender to Him and be forgiven?

Do you really think that's your choice?

You walk through the house and out the front door. The

wind pushes you, rips your hat off and tosses it up into a tree, then knocks it down again and kicks it along the road toward town. It's hotter now. A window smashes, a fence slat pinwheels by, and always the constant fall of ash. Your head smarts and you reach a hand up and touch flame and your hair's on fire. You slap it out, already starting to run.

Fenton's is raging, and the chemist's, Soderholm's, the splash and tinkle of bottles exploding. His windows are melting, the glass like taffy. A swirling wind combs the flaming debris over the street, and before you reach it, the sidewalk in front of Doc's catches and flares up. Your bike leans by the door of the jail, and you dart for it, ignoring the heat. Drag it back, hop on and turn for Ender's bridge, Friendship going up on both sides of you in twin curtains. And here, remember this: you do nothing to save it.

The seat's hot, and it's hard to breathe. The fire thunders, pops like gunshots. You don't stop until you cross the river, and then you vomit, hawk phlegm, hack, gasping. Behind you, the cupola of the livery topples in on itself, the white bell tower smokes, then suddenly erupts.

Why do you always have to look back?

Even here you're not safe. Right in front of you, the roof of Ender's bridge bursts into flame, and you get up on the pedals and ride.

You think you're ahead of it, but farther out the fields are burned over, and patches of forest, weakened trees fallen over the road. A charred deer lies in a ditch, its legs just nubs. Karmann's fence is on fire, and Old Meyer's hives.

Above the treetops, a whirlwind rides alongside you, roaring, casting out flaming shingles and boards, tattered scraps of bills you recognize from Ender's bridge. They light in the fields and run like prairie fire, shoot past you, only slow when they reach a windbreak or the woods' bushy edge. But even there it can catch you, the underbrush is so dry, brittle from a month without rain. You think if you can make the Hermit's lake, you can jump in and let it pass over you.

You think all this, though you know you won't have time.

And then a whoosh and it's on you like a downpour, all around you—a rumbling, and trees crashing down on both sides. You turn the curve and there's the lake. You don't slow, bump hard across the ditch and into the woods. Toss the bike aside and run. The brush stops and then there's nothing but the gray of ash on water. Thorns scratch at your face. You can hear the trees cracking from the heat, the rustle of branches as they fall, and the whump of the earth jumping. And then you're running in the shallows, the water grabbing at your legs, the mud sucking, and you dive and pull for the middle, the sour taste of lye in your mouth.

You stay in the very center, treading water, turning to watch the trees if one should fall your way, drop like an axe on top of you. Through the storm of ash you can barely make out the Hermit's cave on the far shore, but you don't see him. You don't see his ducks either. The reeds are burning. You kick, kick.

Smoke shoulders through the trees, rolls low over the water, and for a minute it's midnight, you're utterly blind, stifled. You cough into your hand, try to breathe. And then it lifts, a gust of wind whisks it off, and the sky brightens until it hurts.

The fire comes suddenly—not from the treetops, as you imagined, but from the brush, driving a fox in front of it. Its coat breaks into flame, it stumbles, and the blaze overtakes it. Pines bend in the heat, strain and creak, the meat of the trunks bursting like cannon. The fire sweeps through, runs up the limbs and leaps to the sky. It comes from the west and follows the wind around both sides, a solid wall, taking everything, scorching your face so you have to duck under and hold your breath. The water warms, turns hot as a bath, and when you have to come up again, your nose is inches from a dead sunfish. You splash it away, and with a slap a tree pitches into the shallows on the far side.

The flames strip the dry pines, send whole branches floating over you, the needles aglow. The water's black as week-old axle grease. The Lake of Fire, you think. If anyone deserves it, it's you.

Yes, a murderer. A lover of the dead.

Take me then, you think.

Do you mean it?

Yet already the fire's moving on, the trees left smoking, the very ground. The rumble comes from the east now, walks off like a thunderstorm. You swim through the fish for the far shore, afraid you might bump into the Hermit, floating facedown, his ducks bobbing beside him, still alive, pecking his head.

You don't. The shallows are hot, and you drag yourself

out, covered with muck. The grass is blackened, even the dirt around the cave mouth. "Hello?" you call, "Hello?"

Pace the bank and peer into the gray water. Inspect the dead logs under the slurry. There's so much ash it's hard to see anything; he could be one of these lumps.

You poke your head into the cave and call again.

You know the smell too well by now, but this is bad. It makes you stop and clap a hand over your nose.

He's in there with his ducks, lying on his back. The ducks are lined up along one wall like decoys, arranged like toys, not a mark on them, and you think, the disease. The fire's touched nothing. It's been a while. His throat is slit, the blood already dried dark on his army bedroll. His head rests on a straw pillow. The knife with the black pearl inlay sits in his open hand, as if he means to return it to you.

Sickness, despair.

But who, you think. Who in the world did he get it from?

And the answer comes to you. That reach across the beaver dam.

So it is you, it's been you the whole time. All of them— Marta, Doc, Sarah Ramsay. It must have been the soldier or Lydia Flynn, then no one but you.

Then why don't you die?

What about the train? Did you kill Bart and Millard for nothing? Or worse, to get it through, spread the infection.

You make your way to the tracks. They're burned over. In the woods, trees are falling steadily, a rush and then a shudder, the ground throwing up a gush of embers, sparks dart-ing like fireflies. You walk along the flickering ties, leaving footprints, your wet clothes binding, grabbing at you. The wind is calm and it's almost quiet, cold even. No birds, nothing. The ashes have stopped falling, and you can breathe easier, each mouthful a cup of water. In the distance, the fire drums, the sky sullen. Already it's far away. The speed of it—you hadn't expected that.

Past the marsh, out along the canal. Bart and Millard are still there, the color of the ground, as if they're part of it. Hairless, their clothes burned off. You'll have to see to them as best you can.

You *are* sorry, but what good does that do?

You walk on toward Shawano, wondering how many of them you spoke with, touched. There's no point—Cyril's in the boxcar, and Harlow, John up front with the driver.

What are you supposed to do, stop them?

Bart tried to.

He was right, you admit, but they're probably halfway to Milwaukee by now.

You'll walk as long as you have to.

You wonder how Kip Cheyney is, if anyone's seen to him, if that doctor's looked at anyone else, someone from town. You remember what Doc said about the epidemic in St. Joe. Half.

Merciful Jesus, you think.

Far ahead, there's something black on the tracks, and you crane to see what it is. It's small, maybe a switching engine. Not big enough to be the freight.

You walk faster, then begin to run.

The black thing is the boiler of an engine. That's the first thing you see.

Closer, you see the stretch of wheels staggered behind the engine, the trucks unconnected to anything, the steel shell of a hopper. Nothing left but metal, the couplings still clasped on the tracks.

You slow to a walk, try not to picture the fire racing the train, the huge wave of flame rolling over it.

So you know even before you see the twisted skeleton of the boxcar. Not that you're ready for it then. If all of this has taught you anything, it's that hope is easier to get rid of than sorrow.

The ground's burned over, and scattered about the right-of-way lie the bodies, curled in the dirt. They're small, and it's not like Bart and Millard, you can't tell who's who. Their hands are just stumps, their faces missing. The children are obvious, the rest of them impossible. You don't bother counting. It looks like they were running for the woods. Didn't get far at all.

John and the driver are still in the cab, the throttle wide open. The shovel in the tender is just a blade, warm to the touch, the handle completely gone. You jump down and walk among the bodies, sit in the dust and ponder them. Cyril's here somewhere, and Harlow, Fred Lembeck. The rest of Friendship.

You still feel a duty to them—owe it, really—and you climb the engine again and bring back the shovel. It's hard but the dirt's loose, and you've got gloves. You're used to work. In Kentucky you did this for weeks.

You remember tending to the little Norwegian, taking great care with him. They all thought he was your friend, that the two of you were inseparable, the way you looked after him, so devoted. You wouldn't let anyone touch him. You buttoned his sleeves so they didn't see the marks on his arms where you stripped the meat off when they were asleep. You said a prayer after you buried him, made another promise to God, instantly became a different man. But did you really change? You thought you had. Now you don't know.

The hardest are John and the driver, who you have to gently let down, their bodies delicate, light as charcoal. And then when you think you're finished, you find what must be the brakeman beside the hopper. You'd all but forgotten him, and silently apologize. It's dusk when you get Bart and Millard in, and full dark when you set the Hermit to rest, his ducks tucked about him like children.

You sit in the cave, opening and closing the knife by candlelight, the Hermit's world spread around you. You've turned the bedroll over, twisted a cigarette to chase the smell of blood. The knife's sharp, and for a second you're tempted. Both wrists, then the throat, deeply.

No. You fold it closed, set it on his dented tin plate.

Because you still believe, isn't that true? Because you do love this world.

You're not sure anymore, are you? It's easier to be by yourself.

No.

Yes. Alone, with no one else. Don't lie, you like it this way.

"No," you say, though it has nothing to do with being humbled either. The whole idea of penance is selfish, misguided. You can't bargain with God, buy Him with pieties. This is what you've found out—that even with the best intentions, even with all of your thoughtful sermons and deep feelings and good works, you can't save anyone, least of all yourself.

And yet, it's not a defeat. After everything, you may still be saved. Your mother was wrong; it's not up to you. It's always been His decision.

You pick up the shovel, blow out the candle and go outside. The moon moves on the lake, stars smeared across a clear sky. The smell of ashes still lingers. Always will, you imagine. You walk in the dark, stumble up through the woods till you reach the tracks. You look east to Shawano, as if a train might be coming, then head for Friendship, the shovel scuffing your leg with every step.

And it's not a mystery to you why you're doing this. It's not a secret. A man who's lost only wants to go home. A pariah, if just some small part of him, wants to belong, to be, in the end, forgiven. Don't those souls in Hell lift their faces to Heaven? Tonight, you think, you need to be with the ones you love.